Praise for
US IN THE
BEFORE AND AFTER

'A masterpiece. A beautiful and breathtaking story of friendship, love and loss, that will shatter your heart into a thousand tiny pieces and then slowly put it back together again.' – Danielle Jawando

'An ode to life and love and loss and friendship – and the devastating beauty of it all. This is the kind of book that grips you by the heart and doesn't let go.' – Katherine Webber

'A gorgeous, heartbreaking and lyrical new YA novel from the wonderful Jenny Valentine about grief, friendship and love.' – Laura Bates

'An absolute page-turner from one of our most vital YA voices. Nobody writes like Jenny Valentine – she is a true original.' – Phil Earle

'A gorgeous journey on friendship, love and death. Jenny Valentine has written a book that you will want to read over and over again.' – Abiola Bello

US
IN THE
BEFORE
AND
AFTER

JENNY VALENTINE

SIMON & SCHUSTER

First published in Great Britain in 2024 by Simon & Schuster UK Ltd

Text copyright © 2024 Jenny Valentine

1 3 5 7 9 10 8 6 4 2

Simon & Schuster UK Ltd
1st Floor, 222 Gray's Inn Road
London WC1X 8HB

Simon & Schuster: celebrating 100 years of Publishing in 2024

www.simonandschuster.co.uk
www.simonandschuster.com.au
Simon & Schuster Australia, Sydney
Simon & Schuster India, New Delhi

A CIP catalogue record for this book is available from the British Library.

PB ISBN 978-1-4711-9658-4
eBook ISBN978-1-4711-9657-7
eAudio ISBN 978-1-3985-1714-1

This book is a work of fiction. Names, characters, places and incidents
are either the product of the author's imagination or are used
fictitiously. Any resemblance to actual people living or dead,
events or locales is entirely coincidental.

Printed and Bound in the UK using
100% Renewable Electricity at CPI Group (UK) Ltd

MIX
Paper | Supporting
responsible forestry
FSC
www.fsc.org   FSC® C171272

For all the ghosts

1. LADYBIRD

We are sitting in the cemetery, me and my best friend, Mab, cracking jokes about the bowling club and how close it is to the graves. I'm drinking warm cider from a can and Mab is chain-smoking these roll-ups she found at the party. Tiny, like dolls' fingers. She stuffed an endless supply in her pockets before the walk home. I remember her face when she was doing it, glowing with fury.

I don't even like them, she says. *But I guess now it's something to do.*

I have stopped trying to decide if all this is the best or the worst thing we could be doing with our summer. It might not be an either/or answer. Mab says maybe it's both. We don't exactly have a whole world of options, I know that much. But I would like to go back to the time before the black hole currently swallowing up my centre was just a pinprick. Just a subatomic particle of loss. I'd go back further if I could. To Before. Before the party, and what happened next. I know everyone would.

Are you still banging on about atoms? Mab says, like she can hear what I'm thinking.

'Nothing changes,' I tell her.

She nods her head. *Even when everything does.*

She is net-curtain thin. Just a veil of herself. Freckles like the start of rain on dry ground, little scar above her eyebrow, bright wet shine of teeth. When I blink, her features drip and spread like running paint. There are drag marks down her right flank, pure tarmac. A rip in her dress, bone-deep. The bruise on her temple is black and shadowed where a piece of her skull has caved in. She turns and grins at me, a mouthful of yellowing smoke. My beautiful friend.

Do you want one? she says, taking a drag.

'No thanks.'

It's honestly disgusting.

'Yeah well. You shouldn't smoke.'

2

She kicks me on the ankle, hard as she can reach, and I want so badly to feel it.

I'm dead already, remember, she tells me. Like I could forget.

It's an in-between time. After exams, before results, when the work's been done, or not, whatever, and it's too late either way. I looked forward to this feeling for so long – like when you've jumped but haven't landed. Nothing left for us to do but wait.

Purgatory, Mab calls it now. *Limbo.*

'Well, you'd know,' I say.

Her arched eyebrow. Grit under the top layer of her skin. *Yep. Quite.*

She keeps waving her hand between us to protect me because she says the roll-ups smell so bad. I tell her not to bother because I can't smell a thing. She frowns, picks a scrap of tobacco off her tongue. Bone-coloured. Bone-tired. It makes me restless just to look at her. I feel bad about the blood still moving, sluggish, through my own veins.

This heatwave has beaten everything into submission. The streets are a film set of themselves. Deserted. Lacking.

'Where is everyone?' I say.

Damned if I know.

I can't help asking her. The question starts in the pit of my stomach, and the only way is out. 'Where's France?' I say. Mab's brother. It's complicated. She gives me a look, and I meet it. I manage to stare her out.

'You still angry about that?' I ask her. 'Really?'

No. She looks away. *I'm over it.* Which is a thing she only tells you when she's not.

It's so quiet. No breeze, no bird noise or traffic. Just the sound of my own thoughts, which are full of him as always, like the sea is full of fish, a clear night of stars. There is dark matter where he used to be. I feel that. A worrying absence of light.

Elk, Mab says, softer now.

'Yes?'

I'm sure he'll come.

I try not to want him. I try hard to get a handle on that.

My little brother moves about in the dry grass below us, snarling and spitting and pouncing, stalking insects like a big cat. He's picking up litter while being a tiger. He's a master multi-tasker like that.

4

Mum hisses at him in a whisper. 'Knox. This is not the place.'

Poor kid, says Mab.

'He's fine,' I tell her. 'He likes it here.'

She stretches herself like she's yawning. *We seem to come here often enough.*

Knox stamps on a crisp packet, adds it to his collection.

He likes the beach better, Mab says.

I watch him growling. The pink of his lip. His perfect little milk teeth.

'He does,' I say. 'You're right.'

The sun beats down, unblinking. I would pay good money for something like a breeze or a downpour right now. One measly piece of ice.

'It's so hot,' I say. 'Are you hot?'

She shakes her head, points her good arm out across the rooftops. The straight lines quaver in the air like they are underwater. It makes me thirsty just to look at them.

Are those the old people's flats?

Towers and turrets and verandas. Lifts and ramps and those emergency switches in the loo. My mum worked there for a while. She said it was relentless.

Looks like Disneyland from here.

Mab rakes her bare heels across the dust. I wonder briefly where her shoes are. Just for a second. Then not.

At least I won't end up there, she says.

'Where, old age?' I picture my gran Joanie. Her tree-root hands and matchstick ankles, her wisdom and her lipsticks and her catchy rattling laugh. 'I could think of worse places.'

Festival toilets, Mab says.

'Pub carpet.'

Your mum's book group.

'Cruise-ship karaoke.'

She laughs at that, and then she stops laughing.

Here.

Mum walks right past us with an armful of old roses, Knox tagging along obediently behind. There's another cider can beside me in the grass. I don't remember drinking two, but it's possible. Maybe I did.

'Don't leave that there,' Mum says, the first thing she's said to me all day.

'I won't,' I tell her. 'I wasn't going to,' and Mab is like, *What is it with you two? What's with your tone?*

Loggerheads. Stalemate. Daggers drawn.

Knox picks the can up for me, bends down close so I can smell his little-boy hair and the midday heat on his skin.

'Put it this way,' I tell Mab. 'Lines of communication are definitely down.'

Mum and I have barely spoken in weeks. I call that her fault, given the circumstances, and I'm too worn out to fix it. I'd say I've got more than enough going on.

My brother catches himself on a bramble, snags his hand on a thorn. The bright bead of blood on his thumb looks just like a ladybird. He holds it up to the light, and grins at me, and licks it off.

Rust, Mab whispers, spellbound. *Iron*.

I think about how she will never taste anything again.

She studies her own hands, bloodless, transparent almost, rings still on her fingers, palely glinting. All except one, the smiley-face signet she found at the beach. Solid gold with black jet eyes. I remember how sorry she felt for whoever dropped it, how well she said she would take care of it, to make up for it being lost. It's mine now. I borrowed it the night of the party, so I'm guessing that's just that. She looks away when she sees me wearing it, like it doesn't belong on my hand.

Did you get a job yet? she says.

'You sound like my dad, by the way, and no, I didn't.'

I miss the cafe. I loved my job.

I rise to that. A total fiction. 'You did not. You complained about the customers, and you said your feet hurt.'

Well, she says. *Nothing hurts now.*

'Does it not?' I ask her. 'Really?'

She looks like she is in pain all the time.

I am watching the ground, the marks her feet should have left. I feel that hollow in my stomach again. The sheer drop. Our new normal. Knox knows how to fill a void. He comes and stands right next to me.

'Where is she?' he says. 'I don't want to tread on her.'

'What do you mean?' Mum asks him, and I say, 'That side.'

He peers, sort of in Mab's direction, and even though he can't see her, she blows him a kiss.

'It's fine, Knox,' I say. 'You won't hurt her. She's good at moving out of the way.'

Mum is using her tight-lipped voice. 'Just stay off the grave,' she tells him. 'Just don't walk on that.' Like that's the only version of Mab up for discussion. Like I haven't already tried to tell her enough times about the fact of my best friend's ghost.

Mab laughs beside me, grimly, quietly. *I hate that she does that. Just denies me.*

'I know,' I say. 'I hate that she does it too.'

The cemetery is massive. Blocks and blocks. All around us the city, and here this other city, marked and labelled, banked in rows and grids like terraced streets. Mum is tidying up the way she does at home – head down, quick-sharp, thinking – with Knox trailing more mess right behind.

'Do you get bad neighbours here?' he says. 'Is that a thing?'

'Bad neighbours?' Mum brushes the dirt off her knees. 'Really. What a question.'

You get nothing and no one, apparently, Mab says. *Bad neighbours would be a plus.*

It's pretty though. Green and peaceful and open, with shady corners and long whispering avenues of trees. A nicer place than many people spend their lives in, this place to be dead.

Some graves have monuments and angels, greening bronze and floral tributes all flattening in the heat, but this one is small and quiet and modest. Not ready yet. Too new for its own stone. There's just this marker in the ground. Hardly worth it. The saddest thing I've ever seen.

'You should have a monument,' I tell her. 'A mausoleum. A skyscraper.'

Not enough, Mab says, her body rising and dropping like waves, like someone else, some larger creature, is breathing her in and out. *Not enough, not enough, not enough.*

Mum yanks at some half-starved daisies. Culling them. Thinning them out. Knox plonks himself down. He is trying to split grass blades and make them whistle, but they are too dry and they just crumple and snap. It's way beyond his skill set. A Herculean task. Mab stares at him intently, the way he presses each one tight, all hope and possibility, between his thumbs.

I say, 'I should get going soon.'

She looks up. *Where to?*

'It's Tuesday,' I tell her. 'I've got Stevie at five.'

She frowns. *You're already going back?*

There's a look in her eye, like maybe she doesn't want the world to keep turning without her. Things in the diary, arrangements getting made.

'I missed two weeks,' I say. 'Plus it's kind of her field, right? Grief counselling. I could do with the help.'

Mab rolls her eyes.

'I was actually hoping you'd be there,' I tell her, and she mimes ending herself, with a knife, with a gun, with a rope.

'Don't do that,' I say. 'Come with me.'

She smiles. Her fractured cheekbone, her heart-shaped chin.

Let's just stay a bit longer, she says. *Let's sit here. Then I promise I will.*

2. CHINCHILLA

Aside from Mab, or what's left of her, I have a mum and dad who still quite like each other, France, who is somewhere, Stevie, my therapist, who is all right actually, and Knox, who has just turned five. My name, Elk, is short for Elena. I know that doesn't make sense the same way Mab does for Mabel and France does for Francis, but that's what it's short for. It is what it is.

We should have left by now, but Mab's not up for moving. I watch her looking at the skyline, all its details. I see her drinking in the light.

I miss everything, she says. *I wasn't ready.*

'I'm sorry,' I say, because there are no better words for it than that.

I wish I had a good book, she tells me, counting some of the things she wants on her fingers.

Fresh strawberries, Elk. I want a strawberry.

A pack of cards.

An ashtray.

'Is that it?'

She was never any good at packing. School trips, when she was sockless. The number of times she forgot her inhaler. The week we went camping and she didn't bring her tent.

At school, when I was much younger, we wrote a list of what we would pack if we had to leave home in a hurry. If war suddenly tried to kill us, the way it does, or famine or flood or a pandemic. All the cheerful things. No wonder children get stressed. I remember our teacher Mr Cressey giving us the options. 'Or if the government passed a law that everyone with blue eyes had to leave,' he said, and all the blue-eyed kids in the classroom being like, 'What?' and all the kids who already got it thinking, 'Yes, even you. Imagine that.'

I hadn't met Mab or France yet. All that was ahead of me. I think about it now, how our lists had phones and cars and family pets and Nintendo on them.

Mr Cressey said, 'No chargers, no petrol, no dog food, no time.'

He said, 'All these things will just slow you down and become useless.'

I think he wanted us to take our loved ones and our passports, at most, and head for the hills.

He was trying to tell us what was important, what might matter, but we couldn't hear him.

I'm listening now.

Mr Cressey got sick and faded away. There was just less and less of him over time until he was gone.

My gran left slowly, head first, top down, forgetting. It was the hardest thing to watch.

Mab went in a matter of seconds. I guess that's why so much of her is still here.

OK then, she says, when I laugh at her wish list. *What would you take?*

Mr Cressey brought a chinchilla to class once. No idea how he got hold of one. We closed our eyes and put our hands out and when we were allowed to look, we were already touching it.

'You can't even feel it,' he told us. 'Because it's that soft.'

I go through the list of candidates. France and

my little brother, my parents and my gran before she died. My comics, my good trainers, all my favourite books. It's a pointless exercise really. I know the answer anyway. I know it before I begin.

I touch Mab's face. I try to anyway. Like the chinchilla, I wait to feel it, and I can't.

'You,' I say, and her eyes are like glass beads, like dew drops, like water. 'One hundred per cent. I'd take you.'

3. SINGLE-USE PLASTIC CUP

It was Mum and Dad's idea that I talk to someone professional. I wasn't into it at all, not to start with. But they kept on at me, in a nice way, and in the end even Mab said it would probably do me some good.

'You can't just sit in the dark reading books about bloody physics for the rest of your life,' she said, and when I asked her why not, she told me, 'Because I miss you, Princess Quantum. I'm dying of boredom over here while you search for your grandma in every black hole.'

Stevie's office is in a rundown building behind the high street. Above a charity shop, next to a dentist. I started going because of my gran. What happened to her really threw me. A slow-motion kind of getting lost, like she was caught in a riptide and we couldn't just swim out and get her; all we got to do was stand there on dry land and watch. I swear I tried, but I couldn't quite seem to let go of it. The whole thing still kind of sticks in my throat.

I actually ended up liking Tuesdays with Stevie a lot. On the way there, I'd think I had nothing to tell her, but inside that room you really couldn't shut me up. The first time though, I didn't know what I was getting into, so I wore all my best armour. I must have been a pretty tough nut to crack. Mum said she was taking Knox to the library round the corner, but I know she only walked me there to make sure I went in. She's quiet like that, but she likes to steer the ship. Sometimes I didn't know she was even doing it, but other times I got wise. My mum is in charge even when she looks like she isn't.

The door stuck on that first appointment, over a year ago now. I had to press the intercom twice and it was awkward, and the carpet needed hoovering on the stairs. There wasn't really a waiting room, just this one chair at the top on its own looking lonely, and some tired magazines that you wouldn't read anyway, even if they were the last magazines left on earth. I was standing there and then the loo flushed at the end of the hallway and this woman appeared. Blouse-wearer. Floral skirt. She was drying her hands on a blue paper towel. I watched how the colour went dark where she touched it.

'Elena?' she said. She had a scar on her throat that inched and wriggled like a flatworm when she spoke. I tried not to stare at it, which meant I couldn't seem to look away.

'Yeah. Sorry,' I said. 'Hi.'

She smiled with her mouth, but her eyes were serious and kind of hungry. 'I'm Stevie,' she said. 'Please, come on in.'

Through the wall, I could hear someone having their teeth drilled.

'That's soothing,' I said, and I thought she might laugh, but she just looked at me over her glasses. Stevie has a plain kind of stare and tattooed eyebrows about three shades too dark. They look like birds flying high in the sky of her face. She also had a notebook and a slight cold that was, she said, 'Nothing to worry about. Do sit down.'

There was a box of tissues on the table next to me, some business cards, a small black alarm clock, and a drink of water in a plastic cup. The coaster underneath it was a close-up photo of a baby duck, and I was in the kind of mood that it annoyed me. On the business cards it said she specialized in grief. Don't we all in the end?

The room was small, and it didn't have that much about it. A bookshelf. A supermarket pot plant. A little rug between Stevie's chair and mine. She told me to make myself comfortable, so I took my shoes off and tucked my legs under me, the way I sit when I'm watching TV at home. It didn't really help.

'So, Elena,' she said.

'It's Elk,' I told her, and Stevie nodded.

'Okay, Elk.'

She did this little introductory pitch about how this was a safe space for me to express myself and talk about what had happened, talk about how I felt. I felt like she'd said that exact same thing a thousand times. I wondered if she was tired of it yet. Then, when the silence had started to feel endless, she asked me, 'What can I do for you?'

I shifted in my seat. 'I don't really know.'

She looked at me for the count of three. 'Why do you think you are here?'

I picked at the bottom of my sock. 'My gran died,' I said, and I knew that didn't even begin to cover it.

Gran had this kind of dementia. At the beginning, she could tell you exactly what happened on a Wednesday in July 1952, and who was there and what they were wearing, but if you asked her what she had for lunch like ten minutes before, she'd stare at you, unmoored, because you were asking her for the impossible. All that past everywhere, and an unknown future, and this elusive, self-cleaning present. Later, 1952 got swallowed up as well. And she didn't just forget things; she forgot how to do things. I think we watched her forget who she was.

Stevie crossed her legs and her tights hissed like something slowly deflating. She said, 'I'm sorry for your loss,' and I probably should have said thank you, but I wasn't feeling grateful, so I didn't say a thing.

'Were you close?'

My jaw was hurting. I felt like a can of soda, after shaking, before someone's cracked open the top. I looked at the door. Gloss paint, old stains, a key in

20

the lock. I guess I could have gone through it. This was meant to be optional after all.

Stevie smiled. I took a sip of water. It tasted like cup.

'Why don't you use proper glasses?' I said. 'These aren't very sustainable, are they.'

'Sustainable?' she said, and raised her sky-bird eyebrows at me.

'Sustainable,' I said again. 'You know. The planet and stuff. Landfill. Pollution. Plastic islands bigger than Texas in the sea.'

'Oh,' Stevie said. 'It's health and safety. Sorry. Hygiene, you know.'

I said, 'You're the one with the cold.'

'Does that bother you?' she asked me.

'Not as much as the cup.'

She looked down at her own lap. 'You're welcome to bring your own water bottle next time. If that would help.'

It's like she gave in so quickly, I didn't know how to feel about it. I took another sip of plastic water. 'I don't actually feel like talking,' I said.

She acted like she wasn't that bothered, the same way we pretend not to care about Knox eating his greens. 'It's your time,' she said. 'You can use it however you like.'

'So, what, I could say nothing?'

'Absolutely. We could just sit here. It's your choice.'

I stayed quiet for a bit. That must have eaten up ninety seconds. A lorry went past outside and the building grumbled. The window blinds swayed like there was a breeze, except there wasn't.

Stevie's clock was like the one my gran had by her bed in the hospice, ticking away the minutes, one by one. By the end, time meant nothing to her. She was a very unpoetic person, but I remember her lying there with the sheets right up to her neck, saying, 'I am the drop returning to the sea.'

I said, 'No one has those any more.'

'What?' Stevie said. 'Alarm clocks?'

'Only old people. Everyone uses their phone.'

'I like it,' she said. 'I guess I'm an old person.'

'How old are you?'

'Fifty-three. Oldish. Medium old.'

You can tell when women start feeling old because they wear neck scarves every day of the year. My mum wore one for a bit, until my brother asked her if she worked for an airline, and my dad nearly

22

choked on his toast. I liked the way Stevie didn't bother with one, even to hide that big old scar. It was raised and slightly shiny, a mended ridge of silk. My gran's neck was twisted paper, a hammock that swung when she talked. Her eyes were crow's feet and cross-stitch from decades of smiling. I thought she was beautiful.

'And you're fourteen, are you, Elk?' Stevie said. She was using my name a lot so I would trust her. Like a sales call. Like a high-value-customer thing.

'Sixteen, Stevie,' I said, and Stevie checked her book.

'My mum is forty-four,' I said. 'My dad's forty-two and my gran was seventy when she died.'

The blinds sliced the view up into neat striped sections. Green paint on the windows and gutters. Old bunting. That blue glass, paint-by-numbers sky.

Stevie waited. I didn't know it yet, but she is very patient.

'You must really miss her,' she said.

At the end of the hour, she suggested I write some things down for next time, so I could feel ready and we could talk about them together. I was tired, biting my nails, and it was like a hothouse in there, like we might be about to run out of oxygen in that sad little room.

'You mean like homework?' I said.

'Yes, if you like.'

I didn't like. Not especially.

Stevie straightened up her little pile of business cards, started gathering her things. The black clock was about to hit the hour and the minute and second.

'Your call,' she said. 'It might be helpful.'

'In what way?'

She stood up, all tidy, with her feet and ankles pressed together. The scar on her neck had gone from silver to pink. 'I'm not here to tell you what to do,' she said.

'Well then,' I said. 'You're literally the only one.'

The dentist was still drilling. Mum and Knox were right outside when I got to the street. Knox had *Not Now, Bernard* and *In the Night Kitchen* under his arm. He was trying to stop them from sliding out of his grip.

I told him, 'You had a much better hour than I did.'

'How was it?' Mum said. She was hoping I was

cured or something, I could tell. Her face was all hemmed in and hopeful. It made me furious.

'Don't meet me next time,' I said, and then I realized I'd just handed her a win right there, because it meant I was going back, and that made me furious all over again. She didn't fight me on it because she didn't have to. She took the books from Knox's outstretched arms.

'Okay, my love,' was all she said.

4. PILOT LIGHT

Mab is a little bit taller and three months older than me. Her hair is long and dark red and heavy, and she smells of fresh laundry, even when she's pulled an all-nighter and ought to stink like a bottle bank, like no sleep and unbrushed teeth. She's interested in every-thing, and she's full of questions; she isn't one of those people who is welded to being right. She's talented, and intelligent, although sometimes she forgets it, some-times she needs reminding. She walks like she knows where she's going, like she has a reason, even when she doesn't. I always thought her world had more colour than mine, better lighting, some kind of point. I've always liked that about her. That and everything else.

In the other world, Before, it was Friday night and we were at her house, in her living room, doing nothing.

She had that glint in her eye, same as always. Like a pilot light. Never out.

'Thingy-Thingy's having a party.'

I was on the floor, playing cards. I had this obsession back then with a game called Once in a Lifetime. You wanted to win it almost as much as you didn't, because once you've won it, you should never play it again.

'Thingy-Thingy?' I said.

'You know. Freya whatshername.'

My heart sank. 'Fisher.'

'Yes,' she said. 'Her.'

Freya Fisher is the kind of person who lives for her phone. Like a thing isn't happening unless it's being documented and getting seen. If Freya Fisher climbed a mountain but left her phone behind, she'd call it a waste of time and effort, like she might as well not have bothered. She wouldn't even enjoy the view. Her life looks totally perfect from the outside, which is why I feel sorry for her. I worry about how she copes when no one's watching. If a tree falls in a forest and all that. I have this picture of her in my head, miles deep at the bottom of the canyon the algorithm has made, yelling for help. I do have a phone. I'm not from another planet. I was just trying to avoid the canyon as much as I could. So, Once in a Lifetime. Maybe to Freya Fisher, I didn't actually exist. A kind of freedom. We can but hope.

'You don't even like her,' I said to Mab.

'True.'

'So why?'

She looked down at herself. 'I mean, there's this.' Hoodie, odd socks.

'You look great,' I told her without even looking, because I didn't need to, because she always did.

'I want to go out,' she said. 'I want to dress up and drink too much vodka and get with someone.'

'You do not.'

'I don't. You're right. But I also actually really do.'

France was upstairs in his room and I was trying not to think about it. Him up there, one wall, one ceiling away. Their parents were out. Mab was stretched across the sofa, arm to arm. She'd painted her nails white, like spilled milk, and I cried over them later.

I said I couldn't think of anything worse than a party at Thingy-Thingy's, and she said that was because I had no imagination.

'Really though,' I told her. 'It's a hard no from me.'

She made a sound, part outrage, part yawning lion. 'Everyone is going to be there.'

'Define everyone.'

'Everyone who's anyone, according to Freya.'

'Yeah, well that doesn't mean very much.'

I looked at her. She could feel me looking. She pointed her toes, flexed her feet, drummed her fingers on her collarbones.

'I'm bored,' she said. 'I mean, what is the point of us being alive if we don't actually do anything?'

What a thing to say. You try and understand irony in English class and then it swoops down in real life and slams you square in the face.

'Harsh,' I told her. 'Unnecessary. We do things.'

'So, prove it.'

'With Freya Fisher's party? Does the proof of it have to be that?'

She sighed, sank down lower on the sofa. 'Well that's what's on offer. I've checked behind door B, and there's honestly nothing else.'

I could hear France walking about above us and the wind shushing and the drip–drip sound of the rain. It was like the weekend had been given an anaesthetic and was counting down slowly from ten.

'One life, Elk,' she said. 'Like that's it. We shouldn't waste it.'

'I'm all good with wasting mine for one night.'

'No you're not,' she said. 'You just don't like parties.'

'You're right,' I said. 'I really don't.'

I looked out of the window. Grey and miserable and wet, but a miracle even still, to be standing there, staring out at the weather. Mab was right, as usual. I could feel her waiting for me to say something, and yes is always a better answer than no.

'I know what you want,' I said, and her eyes were black pools and she said, 'What.'

'One of those nights where we fix the whole world and don't remember how we did it in the morning.'

'I do,' she said. 'I love those.'

'I know,' I said, because I loved them too.

In my purse I had three coins, a scrap of paper and some dust.

I said, 'We're going to have to raid the drinks cupboard.'

'Way ahead of you.'

'And if we get the bus there, we'll have to walk back.'

'France will take us,' she said. 'I've already asked him.'

I watched my own face from the outside. I must be a good liar. I made like the Sphinx or something. I didn't falter. I didn't even blush.

I said, 'Okay, so get up and help me look good then.'

'We're going?' Mab said. 'You're serious?'

'I'm always serious.'

She grinned at me. 'No, you're not.'

I did an impression of her. Quite a good one. *'One life, Elk. Like that's it,'* and she jumped up, covered my hands with noisy kisses, and danced in a tight little circle. A travel-sized victory lap.

'I won't leave your side,' she said.

'Yes you will.'

'I promise I won't.'

She grabbed her phone, turned me round to face the stairs.

'Up,' she said, her voice in my ear. 'Let's get changed. I don't know about you, but I intend to look incredible.'

'When don't you?' I asked her.

'France!' she yelled, when we were outside his door. We could hear him stop moving. I knew he'd been waiting. 'We're going!' And then to me she said, 'Thank you. I'll love you for ever.'

'Yeah, good,' I told her. 'You'd better. You actually should.'

That light in her eyes was sparking, catching. 'You never know, Elk, you might love it.'

Ever the optimist. Always the bright side. I will miss her so much.

5. METRONOME

I met her in a maze when we were eleven. Summer holidays and I went with Mum and Gran to a stately home with endless gardens, banks of colour-coded flowers like stadium crowds, and statues glaring. There were signs everywhere, an ice-cream place and a gift shop. It was a blazing-hot day, like now, but the sun was slightly kinder. We walked past a man on the lawn who said out loud, 'I think I'm more tired than I think I am.'

Mum said she knew what he meant. She was pregnant with Knox and her belly was the moon and her feet were balloons filled with hot sand. She kept frowning down at them, swelling quietly in

33

her sandals like proving dough.

'Not long now,' Gran said, and the butterflies started hatching in my stomach. I didn't know yet how it would feel to have a brother. I had felt the baby through Mum's T-shirt when he kicked.

There were people coming out of the maze with smiles on their faces, so I went in alone. It was fine at first, like a game, where anything might happen, and I was excited for the what. I walked with my hands pressed against the hedges, watched my feet on the pathway, my shadow – me still, but elegant and long. I was aware of my edges, of being solid and alone, like an experiment. I was probably humming. I used to do that quite a lot. The further into the maze I went, the harder it got. I don't think I realized that's the point. There were kids laughing and colliding, grown-ups doubling back on themselves, and a boy told me that if I turned left over and over without stopping, then I'd get out. I hadn't asked him. I guess boysplaining is a thing.

The walls were high, all the lines sharp and definite under the sun. I remember the heat and the cooler blocks of shadow, intermittent, like piano keys. It was all good when I wasn't thinking about the exit, but once I'd started trying and failing to leave, things changed. I turned left, over and over, like the boy told me, but I didn't have much faith in that. I followed people at random, but they all seemed just as lost as me. I kept ending up in this one tight little square with a moss-crusted fountain, an angel dribbling water onto a leaf. I can still remember the sound of that water landing, this blank page blooming in my chest when I heard it, ahead of me, around the corner, again and again. My sense of time started to stretch like old elastic. I wondered what it would be like to be stuck in there for life.

At some point, my elastic snapped, and I gave up and sat on the ground in that little boxed-in square with my back against the base of the fountain. The sky was small and far away, the way it looks in pictures of Manhattan. My shirt was sticking to me, and the moss bloomed crisp and soft across the stone. I picked at the scabs on my knees, and I pictured Mum and Gran going home without me. I wondered if I was hungry. There was a white-noise orchestra tuning up in my head.

Mab walked into my little nightmare and smiled. 'Hello,' she said, and I said hello back, closed up and sheepish and feeble. She must have struggled to hear me. I could hardly get my own voice to leave my mouth.

'Are you okay?' she said.

I shook my head and looked sideways at the dribbling water. 'I can't get out,' I said. 'I just keep being in here, with that.'

She took me seriously and I remember being grateful. 'I got stuck the first time,' she said. 'For ages, but I escaped in the end.'

'How?' I asked her.

She thought about it for a minute, little dip between her eyebrows, tiny flicker at the centre of her chin. 'I don't remember.'

I didn't want to cry in front of a total stranger. I concentrated on holding it back.

'I'm Mab,' she said, sitting on the ground next to me.

'Elk.'

She grinned. 'Elk? Like a moose?'

'Short for Elena.'

'Well, don't worry, Elk.' She opened her hand to show me. Crushed flowers, clustered and felt-tip bright against her palm. 'I left a trail.'

She pulled me up by my hands. 'I was going to use thread like in the story with the minotaur or whatever, but I didn't want to trip people over, and anyway I couldn't find any thread at home, so I just picked these.'

I didn't know what story she meant, but I wasn't asking. She had planned it, and that's what counted. The flowers were our emergency lighting. We followed them like Gretel and Gretel, bumping shoulders and laughing as we went.

'You can eat them,' she said, holding her hand out. 'Try one.'

They tasted like rescue and honey. Perfumed and sweet.

Through the exit, the day opened right up in front of us, the horizon was far away again, and everything was possible. I watched Mab's face under the wide blue sky, and I would have gone straight back in there if she'd asked me to. I think I might have wanted her to ask.

The maze was just us, I guess, and the real world was always going to be different.

Mum and Gran were on a bench by the toilets. Mum had her shoes off and her feet looked deboned against the solid ground, like that chicken cushion thing I will never unsee from the butcher's window. They said I'd only been gone twenty minutes. It felt like way longer than that.

'This is Mab,' I said. 'She basically saved me.'

'Hello,' Mab said. 'I basically did.'

Gran smiled. 'Are you here on your own?'

'No,' Mab said. 'I'm with my brother.'

She pointed to a boy lying on his back on the grass, long legs, knees bent, one arm behind his head. His hair was much lighter than hers, a kind of amber colour, not short and not long. His face was hidden because he was holding a book between himself and the sun. Mab said his name loud enough for him to move it to one side. She waved and he held the book up in a kind of salute, and in the breeze the pages ruffled. In the heat of the day there were little knots of gravel stuck under my shoes where the ground was melting. I remember the palm of his hand, the grass dust between us like plankton in the light, the various creases of his shirt and his trousers and his frown. The book had a cat on the front and it curled up over his face when he went back to reading.

She called him France, and I said, 'What, like the country?'

'I suppose so,' she said. 'His real name is Francis, but he doesn't like it.'

I said, 'I've never been to France.'

'I saw a real wolf there once,' she said. 'Late at night in a campsite, in a forest, so low and quick and crackling I might have dreamed it.'

Gran's smile was like concrete. Mum raised her eyebrows all the way high. I'd never met anyone who talked like that. Like poetry. Unfiltered. Like the honey that comes with the comb.

'You make it sound beautiful,' I told her.

'Well –' she yawned loudly – 'it was.'

'How old is your brother?' Mum said.

'Thirteen.' Mab's eyes burned briefly with fury. 'He's a pig. But only sometimes.'

I remember how he lay still but his foot rocked, up and down, like a metronome. Like a heartbeat. Sixty times a minute.

We sat on the bright lawn just the two of us, and made chains with the flowers and put them on our heads like crowns and stuffed our mouths with petals and laughed till our stomachs ached about nothing

I can remember. When Mum came over, she was holding on to her belly like she thought she might drop it.

'It's time to go,' she said, and I didn't want to leave, but she was hurrying me; she said Gran needed to get home too. Mab waved and smiled. Halfway across the lawn, when I looked back at her, she was lying with her arms out wide, wearing her flower-chain crown, staring flatly at the sky.

'She's very . . . *free range*,' Mum said, like it was a bad thing, like she would prefer a battery kid.

'I like her,' Gran said, squeezing my hand, and I said, 'Yes, me too.'

We were way past the bandstand when I knew I had to go back because I hadn't given her our number. When I told Mum, she looked like she wanted to fall asleep or start crying or ideally both, right there by the gates to the car park, but Gran pushed me gently.

'Go on,' she said. 'Run. And make it quick.'

I was fast. It only took me a couple of minutes. But when I got within sight of the lawn, I couldn't see Mab or her brother. I had lost them. They were already gone.

6. APPLE

It rained for two straight weeks before Freya Fisher's party. Non-stop and so heavy that the roadsides ran like rivers, all fast and muddy-clean. The noise in Mab's bedroom was crow's nest, shipwreck, typhoon. She made a fake-smart comment about Captain Ahab as she smoothed down her new dress.

'Don't give me that,' I said. 'You haven't read *Moby-Dick*.'

Mab stuck her tongue out. 'They all die at the end,' she said, which proved me right.

We left for that party in a downpour, but here we are After, in a graveyard again, pulling clumps of dead grass up by their roots, coarse and dried out and dirty blond, like the man in the twenty-four-hour garage who sold us the cider. Another day, another heatwave. There are hosepipe bans and wildfires and people are gluing themselves to buildings all over the country. The world is evaporating slowly, like if rain doesn't come again soon, we will all do the same and turn to dust.

'I'm burning up,' I say, but Mab looks cold and pale as stone. She smooths her dress down just like Before, straightens the cuffs, adjusts the collar. The fabric is busy – white clouds, high birds, bright cherries. No one else would suit it like she does, but now it is ruined and filthy, clouds blood-drenched, cherries trampled, birds circling. She brushes carefully at all the carnage with her smashed-up hand, takes a deep, unsteady breath, chest lifting, ribs pressing painfully against the pretty cloth. I didn't know that ghosts breathed, but here she is, right in front of me, still doing it.

'You okay?' I say. Stupid question.

She is staring at me. *I can't believe nothing touched you*, she says. *I mean, look at you. Not a mark. Not a scratch.*

I hold my hands out, palms up and empty, feeling

guilty. I don't know what I'm supposed to say to that.

Mab sighs. *Just lucky, I guess.*

I can feel the ground against my back and the taste of the cider, still sour in my mouth. The sky beats down. Boiled blue, perpetual noon. Nothing doing.

Elk, Mab says, and her edges shimmer and crackle. *Do you ever think you're making me up?*

I don't even hesitate. 'What? No way.'

Do you promise?

'I like facts, Mab. You know this. And you are a fact.'

I don't feel like a fact. I feel like nothing.

'Well, you're not.'

You like quantum physics, she said. *There doesn't seem to be lot of fact in that.*

'Quantum mechanics,' I tell her. 'And there is.'

It makes no sense though. Even you said so.

'There are contradictions, maybe. But the numbers don't know how to lie.'

Twenty-one grams, she says. Something we saw on the internet once about the weight of the soul. At the time, she called it nonsense, but she chews on her nails now, eyes soft, middle-distance, hoping it was right.

'A mouse weighs twenty-one grams,' I say, and I have no idea where that came from in my database of useless truths. 'Maybe all mice are ghosts.'

She smiles. *There are enough of them.*

I think of the mice in the walls at Gran's. The way you would only just see them, fast, out of the corner of your eye. The way they multiplied, exponential, when she stopped cleaning and started leaving food everywhere for them, sprinkling it across her own kitchen floor.

'I like having other heartbeats in the house,' she said, and Dad was quiet then, because he knew he hadn't been visiting nearly enough.

Guess what I'm already thinking about, Mab says.

'Go on. Tell me.'

She shakes her head. *Cats.*

Mum is digging on her knees in the dry ground with a little trowel. I watch her rounded back, the soles of her shoes all ridged and dusty, the sun bouncing off the trowel's steel blade. She has a bottle of water, and she keeps pouring it into the hole she is making, to moisten the soil.

Why are we here again anyway? Mab says.

'I was going to ask you the same question.'

44

Why's she bothering with all this upkeep and stuff? she asks me. *Who's it even for?*

'She tidies for pleasure,' I tell her. 'You know that. Plus she loves you.'

Loved me.

Knox is watching. That boy doesn't miss a thing. He puts his little hand on the dry mound of earth, pats it, kind of comforting, whispers, 'I love you.'

Mum is planting pansies, soft and clustered. Mab looks at them and smiles and licks her lips. It could have been a lifetime ago or only yesterday that she found me lost in that maze, and it feels exactly like both. I can hear an ice-cream van somewhere, out of sight and getting closer, its tune warped and lurching like music played underwater. Mab follows the sound of it with her eyes, seeking it out. Knox jumps up and takes off running and Mum sits back on her heels to watch him go.

I'm so hungry, she says.

'You're always hungry.'

Aren't you?

'No. Not right now.'

She pulls a face. *I'm starving. Distract me. Tell me something. Anything. Quickly. Now.*

'Did you know,' I say, 'there was a time when sailors had no idea of where they were on the planet's surface. Before compasses and constellations. Before north and south and east and west.'

Her arms are tight round her stomach. Her jaw is tight. We can see out across the rooftops and the fading grass and Knox, running for ice cream, getting closer and closer to the fence.

This isn't the ocean, Elk.

Daylight shines on her hair and the bones of her face, whole continents of bruising beneath her skin, the blood turning brown and red and gold like autumn. She is good at telling me what this isn't. The first time I asked her to describe it, she thought really hard for a minute. I could see her thinking, that *v*-shaped dip in her brow, her fingers leaning against each other, pressing inward like a steeple. She pointed to an apple on the table, red, shiny, a world away from her, unreachable, reflecting the day's sharp light.

In that apple is a window, she said. *And through that window is a whole other world.*

Like that straightened it out.

*

This will be my twenty-eighth session with Stevie. My first one since what happened to Mab. I don't know how she will feel about me bringing Mab's ghost along. It's not like I exactly have a choice. But I've never seen anything faze Stevie, so I doubt that this will be it.

Mab smiles. *Are you going to tell her about me then?*

'I tell her everything. That's kind of the point.'

Will she believe you?

'I don't know. I hope so.'

She gets to her feet. *Let's go then.*

The sun burns feverish as we leave the cemetery and come out from under the soft protection of the trees. All the light of the day travels through her, like when you put your hand over a torch and watch it glowing. Mab is stained glass. She is lit up from within.

I say, 'You'll like her. I'm glad you're finally going to get to meet.'

Fingers crossed, she says, as we go through the gates and out onto the busy, living street.

The ice-cream van is pink and white, and when we get closer to it I can see it's coated in a fine layer of soot and exhaust fumes and dust. Someone has drawn a broken heart on the back. Knox is trying to be tall enough to see over the counter. His shorts pocket jangles with change. Next to the bins there is a dropped lolly.

Tragic, Mab says, staring at it. *That is tragic.*

It is peppered with kerb dirt and insects. Mab touches her lips. Her mouth looks so dry.

'You can't have it,' I tell her.

I know that, she says, still staring, helpless, as it melts stoically into the ground.

7. GHOSTS

In Stevie's waiting room, Mab looks at the magazine covers and growls somewhere deep in her throat.

People waste their time alive doing nothing, she says, and I figure she only says it like that, with such venom, because she is dead.

'We wasted enough of it,' I tell her. 'We were quite happy doing that.'

I'd be smarter about it if I got it back.

I think of the book I read once about a man who got to live his whole life again, from the moment it went wrong, like he thought he could do it better, but he just repeated the same mistakes over and over. I can't remember the man's name or what the book

49

is called. Like my gran, in her last weeks, I can only remember the feeling. That book made me sad.

Mab stands up straight and looks down at me in my one single chair. It's right by the banister, and if I lean to one side, I can see down the stairs to where the mail is all piled up on the ground floor. For less than a second I feel giddy. The floor buckles and the ceiling swoops, and then it rights itself and the feeling is gone.

'What are we doing here?' I ask her.

Feeling for the bottom? Mab says.

'If there is one.'

She nods. *It might be a long way down.*

Someone is talking on the other side of Stevie's door. A man. Droning on. And running late. His time should be up already. I'm sure it's after five o'clock. I can't hear what he's saying and I'm glad about that, because I think of the next person, waiting, trying to listen through the door to me.

Shall I go in and spook them? Mab says, and I think about how hard it is sometimes, sitting there spilling your actual guts up for Stevie to consider, and I say, 'No, leave them alone. They'll be done soon. Let's just wait.'

They wouldn't notice me anyway, she says. *Nobody does.*

Which is true. She has a point.

There's a low stack of paper on the table if you want to write things down before your session. I've found it quite helpful, off and on. I take one of the magazines to lean on, write Mab's name at the top of the page and underline it like an essay heading, and then I stare at the paper and my head just empties, the way it does when I go into a bookshop and forget the title of everything I've ever decided I want to read. I chew on the end of my pen. Saliva. Hot plastic. I can see the cover of the magazine through the empty paper. *Summer Issue. Retro Bedrooms.* Some million-dollar hideaway. Everything feels meaningless and all of it is a shame.

Mab moves around the room, urgent but aimless, the way a wasp does. She is whistling.

I say, 'Shall I write, "She's quite annoying when she's bored"?'

Sure. Right after, 'She has no friends, and her jokes aren't funny.'

'You have loads of friends,' I tell her. 'People love you.'

She smiles at me. *I think I'm pretty funny too.*

I can't get started. It feels a bit like writing a diary, like when I read it back I don't know if I'll recognize my own voice. I don't know if I'll like it. I've never been any good at all that.

Will you ask her where I can get some ghost skills.

'What skills?'

I don't know. Shoplifting. Blood curdling. You know, making people jump and stuff. Like in her line of business, she might have contacts, you know.

'I'm not writing that down,' I tell her.

Suit yourself.

My pen on the paper sounds scratchy, mouselike, and I wonder if I should ask Stevie about my mouse-ghost theory, if it's the sort of thing she might like. I go over the letters of Mab's name a bit harder, until they are raised like Stevie's scar on the back of the paper, until they've made grooves in the cover of the 'Homes to die for' magazine.

I didn't think it would be this boring, Mab says.

'What? Dying?'

Haunting.

'I'm sorry.'

I didn't think I would feel so trapped.

The sounds behind the door change. The session is ending.

Time's up, Mab says, and she starts doing a *Countdown* noise by the door. I get another wave of grief then, a real roller. I drop my pen and bend down to pick it up and the blood rushes to my head. I hate crying, so I'm not going to do it. I'm a jar with a lid on. I don't want to overflow.

What's wrong with you? she says.

'The usual.'

When my dad is bothered about something, he turns it into a balloon and lets go of it, watches it float up and drift off and leave him alone. In my mind his balloon is always red. Sometimes he does it behind Mum's back when she's having a go at me. It makes me smile at just the right moment, and on a good day it makes her smile as well. My dad is an expert tension breaker, although these days even he is struggling to do that.

I let go of my balloon in the waiting room, but it just hits the ceiling and stays there.

'Nothing new,' I say to Mab. 'I just miss you.'

I'm right here, she says, and she winks, and my heart breaks again, and she blows me a kiss.

Stevie and the droning man come out. He is middle-aged and kind of colourless apart from his eyes, which are pink like a rabbit's from crying. He's cleaning his glasses and blinking a lot, like he's come from the dark into light. He stares at Mab without seeing her. I don't even think he notices me. Stevie has his plastic cup in her hand. It's filled up with tissues. She looks like she needs a holiday, honestly. I smile. I flick my doodled-on paper with my index finger. It makes a satisfying thwacking sound.

'Mind how you go,' she says, but the rabbit-eyed man looks like he's past caring. I don't think he'd mind if he fell down the stairs and broke his own neck.

Stevie looks in my direction and then disappears into the bathroom. The man has a grey coat and as he goes down, I can see the start of a bald patch on the top of his head.

That is one sorry human being, Mab says, and you can feel it in the stairwell like petrol fumes, like smog. *Guilty as charged.*

'Do I do that?'

Do what? Mab asks.

'Fill a whole house up with how I'm feeling.'

She smiles at me. *Depends on who you ask.*

I have this image of Mum and Dad and Knox in a place after I've left it, throwing open the windows, trying to get some air. I think of my gran and the lightness she always brought with her, even at the end.

Mab is still watching him. He fumbles with the door handle, presses himself up against the wall before he steps out. *Stevie's got her work cut out with that one.*

'Well, she's good at what she does.'

Imagine her life though, Mab says. *Wall-to-wall grief counselling. Five bathroom breaks a day.*

'She only works Tuesdays and Thursdays.'

I bet she drags it around with her seven days a week.

When Stevie comes back, she's got a cup of herbal tea. Just one. She knows I don't like it.

'A proper mug,' I say, and she sighs, tired. 'No plastic.'

She sits down heavy in her chair like a sack, breathes out through her mouth, cradling her hot cup. 'What a day,' she says.

Mab lays herself out like a corpse on the rug. She seems to think that's funny. I watch her for a minute, watch the rhythmic rise and fall of her chest, and Stevie watches me. Nobody says anything. It's kind of peaceful.

Mab stays still for about four more seconds before she gets up and starts moving about.

Restless legs, she says, and she looks over Stevie's shoulder at her notebook. *That man's name was Rigby. Yours isn't in here.*

'I'm a regular,' I tell her. 'She calls me Elk.'

Stevie shuts the book and puts it on the table. The clock is ticking. She steeples her fingers together.

'So,' I say.

I'm not sure where to start really. So much has happened. I'm in my own black hole.

Mab points at my piece of paper. There are craters in it where I've pressed too hard with the pen.

How's your list going? Can she see it?

'No,' I say to Mab. It's not really anything. 'There's no point in seeing it yet.'

She peers through the slats in the blinds at the road below. *Well, these are dusty.*

'She has other priorities.'

I guess we can't all be your mum.

Stevie is wearing very sensible sandals and tights

the same colour as her skin. The seam runs across the tops of her toes like another scar. Mab's scars look like torn fruit in comparison, mouth-flesh, a livid, pomegranate red. Her left shoulder hangs there, dislocated, like a broken wing. Her fingers are dirty and bleeding, and the soles of her feet are caked with wet mud, but she doesn't leave a mark on anything.

I can't believe this is my afterlife, she says.

'It isn't,' I tell her. 'It can't be. Yours would be so much better than this.'

If there even is one, she says, crossing her fingers on her good hand. I think about how that must feel for her – one death and still, the chance of another. I think about how she bears all that weight.

'How have you been?' I ask Stevie, and Mab says, *Isn't she supposed to ask you that?*

She is going through the bookshelf. *These are a laugh a minute.*

'You're funny,' I tell her.

Well, somebody needs to be.

She swings her arms, clicks her fingers. Mab was never any good with silence. *What are you supposed to talk about?* and I tell her, 'Whatever I like.'

What, so you could discuss earthworms for sixty minutes?

57

I look at the little clock. 'Fifty-three minutes now, but yes. It's up to me.'

Are earthworms hermaphrodite? Mab says. *Is it true that if you chop them in half, they carry on living as two?*

'Do you want me to ask that?' I say, and Mab goes, *No.*

Do you think her real name is Stephanie or Steven? What do you think her home life is like? Does she like crochet? Does she watch true crime. Does she have cats? I'm saying she has cats.

I have never thought about Stevie's life outside this office. I take her questions as proof that Mab is a nicer person than me.

Go on then, she says. *Let me see you in action.*

'Mab died,' I say, and Mab goes, *Wow. Jugular*, and Stevie looks at me in a way that's so much better than the usual, you know, sorry for your loss. I think that she would get up and hug me if she could, if it wasn't on some list of violations of her ethical code.

'It's why I missed our last few appointments,' I tell her. 'I came back as soon as I could.'

Stevie has her eyes closed. 'Oh, Elk,' she says, and I can tell by her voice that she's feeling it. That she thinks she understands where I'm at. So I figure it's now or never. I have to tell her.

'She's also right here,' I say. 'Like, her ghost is. I'm talking to her right now. In my head. Well, somewhere, I guess.' I smile at Mab. 'And she's still doing most of the talking.'

Tell her I like her shoes, Mab says.

'She says your blinds are dusty.'

Stevie laces her fingers together, puts her knuckles to her chin. This is her code for keep talking, for when she doesn't want to interrupt your flow.

'She's here,' I say. 'And nobody else can see her and my mum's pretty much given up on me and it's like my gran all over again but worse, which I can't believe I'm saying, but – I don't know. It's Mab. And it was so quick.'

Mab says, *You know when you're a kid and adults talk about you like you're not in the room.*

'Yes.'

This is like that.

Knox hates it as well. His face goes all still like he's hiding until it's over. 'Sorry,' I say.

'I'm sorry,' Stevie says now, shaking her head, tears in her eyes.

Does she just repeat stuff? Mab says. *Like if you said,*

59

'chicken', she'd just go 'chicken'. Or if you said, 'bite-size' or 'post-it' or, I don't know, 'Armageddon', she'd just say it right back at you, like an echo?

'She's a good listener,' I tell her. 'It's not about what she says. That's not her job.'

Oh sorry. Carry on then, Mab says. *Don't mind me.*

'I know you don't "believe" in ghosts,' I say to Stevie, and I do that bunny-ears thing with my fingers around the word *believe*, and instantly hate myself for it. I mean, who even does that? I didn't think it would ever be me.

Stevie's face is all questions. We have talked before about the traces of other people's sessions in the building, past words and past feelings, her own idea of ghosts. She gets up and goes to the window, which is unusual. I think she's worn out, and I don't blame her. We'd been making such good progress before this. Now she must feel like we're back to square one. One step forward, ten steps backwards, or something like that.

'It's a lot,' I say. 'I know. I just need to talk about it.'

Stevie sits back down. She sips her tea. I can smell it. It reminds me of having a cold.

I open my mouth and I don't stop until the clock

makes me, until our time is up. Even then it's hard. I tell Stevie what happened and she doesn't interrupt me once. Even Mab is quiet, which is unheard of, like an actual world first. She sits on the little rug with her chin in her hands, listening.

I catch myself thinking they're a pretty good audience. I only wish I had a better story to tell.

8. PENCIL CASE

The second time Mab and I met was September, the start of year seven and all its firsts, all its possible horrors. I didn't have time to be nervous. In the weeks between, Knox was born, a bawling grenade, and our house exploded. Suddenly, family life was nothing but noise and frayed edges and endless laundry, cold takeaways and spreading patches of sicked-up milk. I had a dream that we took him shopping and came back with a pumpkin instead of his head.

'A baby's a big responsibility,' Mum said when I told her, and Dad said, 'At least one of us is getting some sleep.'

I heard them whispering at night in the living

room about whether I was 'taking it well' and I told them to please talk about something else and that I was fine. I said, 'I do love him, the little dirtbag,' and Dad said that was good, because in that case, the dirtbag could stay.

I spent a lot of time with Gran around then. Back when she could still be trusted not to leave all the taps running, or start a fire in her own kitchen, or hurt herself doing something harmless, or go out and get instantly lost.

'Leave them to it,' she told me. 'You're my best girl. Let's get out in the world and have some fun.'

Luckily, our idea of fun was the same. It was Gran who taught me about the constellations, showed me how to use a telescope and took me out in the middle of the night to get the best of it. It was Gran who bought me my first book about quanta, and the Einstein poster I still have on my wall. Not everyone's cup of tea, I get it, and Mab was never slow to point that one out, but oh, it was so very definitely mine.

My gran studied physics at Cambridge. She said she was one of only four women in her year.

'Science is not confined to the lab,' she told me. 'It is a way of thinking and looking at the world.

'I like that,' I said.

'Tell Chien-Shiung Wu,' she whispered. 'She said it.'

On the first day of term, I'd left half my stuff at home by the front door. I was stressed because we hadn't filled in the right forms, and we couldn't even find them. The lost forms were the reason I was late. The lady in the school office had sharp corners and fast questions. She wasn't exactly welcoming. My mum would have called her a judgey cow, to her face, and my gran would have backed her up too. I was glad nobody came to school with me any more.

The classroom walls were pale blue. The desks were grey with metal legs, and messages in biro that said *RE Sucks* and *BRADLEY BRADLEY BRADLEY* and *If Ever ThEn NOW*. The doorframe was chipped and glossy white and Mab walked right through it. Calm and certain, the same way she walked into that maze.

'Sorry I'm late,' she said, in a way that made it clear she wasn't really.

It was like a second chance at something. My heart was pounding; the smile felt like a sunburst on my face. I stood up and waved at her. Both hands.

'Oh my god,' she said, and she came straight over, put her pencil case on the desk next to mine, like someone planting a flag on Everest, or at the point of the South Pole. The day opened right up in front of us, the horizon was far away again, and everything was possible.

'Elk,' she said, with her arms tight around me. 'I don't believe it. It's you!'

She hugged me and she didn't let go. She was holding on to me like I was a kite that might fly away. The teacher was saying something about water bottles, something about phones. His name was Mr Elliot, and he had a stinking hangover. I'd heard him telling one of the year-ten teachers in the hall.

'What did I miss?' Mab said, when we finally sat down.

I couldn't take my eyes off her.

'Nothing much,' I said, and I meant it, because suddenly it felt like real life had only just begun again. 'Nothing really at all.'

Mr Elliot's hangover turned out to be kind enough to let us talk amongst ourselves in registration. It was

Mab who told me all the things I needed to know, like where the dinner hall was, and the quickest way between classes. The right place to be in the playground. The teachers you could and couldn't trust.

She said, 'Year sevens aren't allowed in the downstairs toilets. They are out of bounds for us.' She said, 'Mr Elliot is a pushover, apparently, but stay away from Miss Bartlett and Mr Winger if you can help it.'

'How come?' I said.

'Strict,' she told me. 'Bad cop and bad cop.'

'How do you know all this stuff?' I said.

'France has been training me all summer.' She touched the side of her nose. 'Inside information and that.'

I thought about her brother on the grass, and the country with the wolves in it.

'I came back for you,' I told her. 'But you were gone.'

She put her hands on her cheeks, like in horror. 'Wait until I tell him you turned up,' she said.

'Why?' I said. 'What will he do?'

She put her head to one side. 'He'll be happy about it, of course. He'll be very pleased, for me.'

She wrote down my address and phone number

three times and put one in her pencil case, one in her shirt pocket, and the last one in the toe of her shoe.

'I can't fail,' she said. 'I've got back-ups.'

'We'll be here again tomorrow,' I said. 'And pretty much every day after that.'

'I know,' she said, smiling. 'It's the best thing that's happened. And I'm not losing track of you ever again.'

9. GRAFFITI

On the phone to mine that weekend, Mab's mum said that Mab hadn't stopped talking about me since day one, and did I want to come over and stay the night. Her name was Joss and Mum could hardly hear a word she said because Knox was crying like his life depended on it; I guess maybe because it did. I hadn't slept away from home before. No one had ever asked me. I packed a bag, but I didn't know what to put in it. A toothbrush and pyjamas. A book, I think. A bar of chocolate from the fridge.

On Saturday, Dad pushed Knox's pram up the hill with my bag stowed in the bottom. Knox was asleep, and Dad said it was a while since he had heard the smaller things, like birds, or the leaves on the trees. 'Or my own voice,' he said. 'Or the thoughts in my head.'

I said, 'Was it like this when I was a baby?' and he laughed and said, 'No. You were our first, so it was way, way worse.'

We stayed quiet after that. We listened. To the wheels on the pavement, a vehicle reversing, the gulls, and our footsteps, a small plane flying somewhere, out over the sea.

Mab lived in Florence Gardens. Dad whistled when we got to the corner. Wide and leafy and pin-drop quiet, filled with sky and wedding-cake buildings, all pastel and tree trunks and piped icing. Same town but a million miles from our town. Another world, honestly, from ours.

'You don't half pick them,' he said, but I knew already that Mab had picked me.

The house was the last one on the right, the biggest and the whitest. The closer we got, the less spotless it looked. It had no name that I knew of, no number we could see. Its roof and walls patched up and all leaning this way and that. There was a cupboard screwed on the front wall for mail and a dusty red car parked so close to the house that it looked like part of the building. I saw a room through a window that had been left open. Bird's-egg blue and empty of furniture, with a small high window like a cell, sunshine streaming on a pot plant, sharpening the saw-toothed edges of its leaves. Outside, high-blown hedges, a big, dense, untamed triangle of garden, a red-and-pink gate lolling off its hinges like a tongue. Through the gaps in the leaves, bright fractions of mismatched chairs clustered in gossipy factions. There were bottles in the grass like wildflowers. A willow tree that looked like it was really weeping. I opened the gate and Dad pushed the pram through. I could hear people, but we couldn't see anyone at first. Only voices, like a party, and someone playing *When the Saints* on the trumpet, over and over again.

Dad said, 'Are you sure this is the right place?' and I wasn't sure of anything, until Mab came bursting through the door like a missile in a bright yellow tracksuit. She hugged me and danced around us and when she put her face up close to Knox's, Dad went very still.

'His breath smells so clean,' she said, searching for the right words, 'like fresh air, and sweets.'

My baby brother flinched in his sleep, the way you do when you're falling.

'Startle reflex,' she said, and I said, 'Really?' I'd never heard about that.

'Imagine,' she said, and the light bounced off her smile, 'what babies must dream.'

All the weeks Knox had been alive, I hadn't thought about that. It was a gift to have Mab translate the world into her language, so I could see it the way she did. It was an honour from the beginning, for me.

She sniffed him like a flower, and Dad said, 'Easy there,' not half as impressed as I was. 'Let's not detonate anything. Let's try not to anger the beast.'

Mab's mum came out of the house to meet us. There was paint on her sleeve and she wore these fine gold bracelets that winked and glittered in the sun. She put her hand on my shoulder when she was talking, and she smelled of jasmine and turpentine and cut grass. Dad rocked the pram back and forth to keep Knox asleep.

'Be good,' he told me when he hugged me. 'Be yourself. I love you. Have fun.'

He rattled the pram back through the gate and

71

along the pavement, getting quieter, crossing the road. I considered worrying for an instant, and then Mab pulled me with her, through the door and into the house. It was dark and kind of blinkered after the outside, like that gathering feeling you get right before you pass out. We took our shoes off and skidded around on the polished floor in our socks. I can hear it now, like it's happening, that quiet sound of us. The place was like a gallery or a museum. There was a lot to see on every wall and I saw all of it. My gran called it using your eyes by closing your mouth. The banister on the staircase was dark and polished and it ended in a tight curl like an early fern, like a clenched fist.

I followed Mab into the kitchen, which was stacked with saucepans and blenders and other equipment, chopping boards and sharp knives and a load of cookbooks high up on a shelf. On the counter there was a huge fruit bowl, overflowing, and pots of fresh growing herbs. Something that smelled good was bubbling gently on the stove. The whole of our downstairs could have fit in that one room. There was a long table down the middle, and two of everything – two ovens, two sinks, two fridges. It had never occurred to me that one of each might not be enough.

'My dad's a chef,' she said.

'And your mum?' I said.

'She's a painter. She can't cook at all.'

France came in and started going through one of the fridges. He was wearing a black shirt and shorts and tennis shoes with holes in them. I watched him, and Mab watched me.

'See?' she said. 'I found her.'

'Like treasure,' he said, and laughed. 'X marks the spot.'

He leaned on the counter opposite me. 'What's your name again?'

Mab spoke before I did. 'It's Elk.'

He smiled. 'That was it. Elk.'

He bit into an apple, almost broke it in half. His teeth were white and very even.

'She hasn't stopped talking about you, Elk,' he said.

'You were lost,' Mab said, with her hand on my arm. 'And I found you.'

'I was,' I said, finding my voice at last. 'And you did.'

★

There was a wall in the sitting room that Mab drew on, down low, behind the sofa. A disembodied head on the skirting board. A tree dropping leaves to the floor. A box tied with a bow and a fork-tongued snake. I wrote my name on that wall. I did a very bad picture of a horse. I wanted to rub it out and start again, but I couldn't. It wouldn't come off.

Her dad had the kind of shoes I could hear coming like a drum kit, like a hard clap. The sound of him made me sit up straight, like I might get told off for the graffiti, but he wasn't like that. Big hands, strong voice, soft face, a sort of *tick-tick* in his jaw.

I said, 'Thank you for having me,' because that's what Mum had told me to say, and he put his hand on my head like a blessing. His skin smelled of jasmine too.

Her bedroom was in the attic. Darker than night, because of these blackout blinds, and warm as toast because the walls were lined with long, thick curtains. 'From an actual stage,' she said, and I thought about all the people who had seen them before us, all the things that had gone on behind.

A light on the floor spun the planets and stars out onto every surface, deeply silent, gently turning. She still has that light five years later, although the books on her shelves are different, the pictures have been changed too. If what I've read has any truth in it, all the cells in our bodies have been replaced by new ones in that time, which makes me wonder if we are even the same people at all.

'I'm not scared of the dark any more,' she said. 'I used to be, when I was little.'

I still was, but I didn't tell her that.

'I'm a bit scared of your brother,' I said instead.

She giggled at that. Little high notes in the deep dark. 'No you're not.'

'And shark attacks,' I said. 'And dying.'

Her voice was this spark in the corner, facing away from me, out in space. 'Shark attacks won't get you, but dying definitely will.'

'I know,' I said. 'It's not that so much. It's more the not knowing when.'

'Oh,' she said. 'I wouldn't want to see it coming. That would ruin everything, for me.'

It was the first sleepover of hundreds. I loved staying at Mab's house as much as she loved staying at mine. We were in the same classes at school. I'm so glad we were never apart if we could help it, from the beginning to the end.

Gran said we were the definition of the word *inseparable*. She said, 'In physics, you call it entanglement. And you're entangled particles, the pair of you. You exactly correlate.'

'I don't understand that,' Mab said. 'But I know that it's true.'

Every day we learned something new about each other. We compared ourselves. My hair was dead straight, and Mab's wasn't. Her nose was narrow and fine, and mine always seemed to be ahead of me like the prow of a ship. I could curl up my tongue at the sides like a taco, and she couldn't, but she could raise one eyebrow without knowing she was doing it, and I would give myself a headache failing while she was like, 'No, no, are you even trying? No, that's definitely not it.'

When we found a common thread, we crossed it like a bridge to celebrate.

We both hated the knot in an egg. The belly button, Mab called it as she dragged it to the side of the plate. We were enthusiastic dancers. We both slept lying on our right side, with our knees tucked up and our left arm in front of our right. We found the same stuff funny. We found most stuff funny when we were together, I think. Mab made a point of enjoying a thing, everything, if at all possible. It was one of her few rules of life. We hummed when we were busy. We cared about dogs and old people and recycling and each other. Mostly each other, before everything else.

There was a vein that stuck out in the soft place at the back of each of our right knees. It was worm-thick and it broke the surface for about an inch before it dived down again out of sight.

France has one exactly the same. The first time I saw it, we were in the garden at their house, summer of year ten, and he was sleeping on his stomach, passed out in the afternoon sun.

'Mab, look,' I said, and I pointed to it.

They had been arguing. Something about a charger and a door hinge. Nothing important. It never lasted.

She said, 'That's the only thing I've got in common with him right now.'

France turned his head and opened his eyes, all drowsy and grass-flecked.

'We've got loads in common,' he said, smiling.

'It's true,' I said. 'You do.'

'We've got the same vein,' Mab said.

France reached down and touched the back of his leg.

'I know,' he said. 'Hasn't Elk got one too?'

'We're like the black-hand gang,' Mab said. 'Except what are we?'

'The worm-knee club?' I said, and their fight was officially over, and France rolled onto his back and looked up at me while he laughed.

I never saw a vein like that on anyone else, and not because I wasn't looking. Knox doesn't have one. Nor do my mum and dad. I've been at the packed beach in high season and there hasn't been a vein like that in sight.

Just us then in our gang, with our built-in flaw. I often thought that if you took a blade to that vein, if you were so inclined, you could bleed the three of us dry.

10. CLOCKS

In the quiet of Stevie's office, Mab asks me to pick up
a shell from the windowsill. I haven't seen it before.
Maybe the rabbit-eyed man left it. I hold it in my
palm, smooth and cool.

'This is nice,' I say, and Mab sighs beside me,
softly. Jealous. *Yes.*

Put it to your ear, she says. *Can you hear the sea?*

What I hear is Mab. Breathing. Slow and deep
like when she's asleep. She goes out so fast, like a
light. Like falling off a cliff. Here and then gone. I
used to lie awake and envy her that.

I say to Stevie, 'If there's no one waiting outside,
I have one more thing,' and she leans forward to

listen. The room is warm and the mood is soft and Mab is content and blinking slowly, like a cat.

'I've been thinking about time travel,' I say. 'Or well, about how there's really no such thing as time.'

Stevie leans back again. Mab looks at me like she always looks when I get started on this stuff.

'Hear me out,' I say. 'I just mean it's possible, theoretically, for Mab to be in more than one moment at once. Like that's proven, I think. Mathematically.'

Go on, Mab says, and I do a double take. Like, 'Really?' because she has one hundred per cent never said that to me before when it comes to this. *I'm listening.*

'So like she's not a ghost,' I say to Stevie. 'You know, in the Victorian kind of ectoplasm meaning of the word.'

No thank you.

'But she's proof.'

Of what?

'That the universe is here and isn't. That it does and doesn't make sense.'

Stevie doesn't say anything. I don't really need her to. She's a mirror in these sessions. To reflect what I'm saying. With Stevie, you end up working things out for yourself.

★

I remember the time when Mab took my little brother time-travelling. He was four and I had to babysit and Gran was a no-go by then in terms of childcare, so I took him to Mab's house on the way home from school.

'How four are you?' she asked him, and Knox thought long and hard about the question and told her, 'Just.'

She said that he was twenty-eight in dog years, but he didn't believe her. We were all still standing in her hallway, and he narrowed his deep-water eyes at her and said, 'A year is the same for everyone.'

'Well yes,' I said, 'that's true. But it also isn't though.'

Mab rolled her eyes. She put her hands over Knox's ears because she knew what was coming.

'Don't lecture your tiny brother,' she said, but Knox didn't need protecting from me. He liked this stuff.

'Why isn't it?' he said.

'Because time passes differently, depending how close you are to the ground.'

His frown. His thinking face.

81

'Einstein's special theory of relativity?' France said, on his way past.

'Don't start,' Mab told him. 'Please god, don't the two of you get into this.'

France laughed, but he stayed where he was and I carried on. 'Like, if you put one twin by the sea and one on top of a mountain, time would pass more quickly for the twin higher up. In the end, he would be a tiny bit older than the other one.'

'Why won't you let them be together?' Knox said. His chin back then was about the size of a thumbprint, no bigger. 'Twins won't like that.'

'Good question,' Mab said. 'Good point. Science is so cruel.'

'It's just a theory,' I told him. 'You wouldn't actually do it.'

'Dogs are closer to the ground than we are,' Knox said. 'But some are taller than me.'

Mab was smiling at me. 'Are you just making this stuff up?'

'Honestly,' I said, 'the closer to the earth you are, the slower time goes. Not by much at all for us, like you couldn't measure it, but still. If you times it by the kind of distances you get in space, you start getting somewhere.'

'Poor defenceless little kid,' Mab said. 'Do you get this a lot, Knox?'

Knox got it all the time. He said, 'What distances?' and you could see his tongue stumbling over his teeth when he said it.

'Like one second on earth being two million years in some far corner of the universe,' I said, and Knox was still for a second while he heard it. Then he blinked.

France was smiling at me like he wanted to say something.

'What?' I said.

He shook his head. 'I didn't know you were interested in physics. I was enjoying listening to you.'

'She's obsessed,' Mab said. 'Same as you are.'

'I had no idea,' he said. 'Can you explain Schrödinger's cat to me next?'

'Probably not,' I said. 'But I could give it a go.'

France shook his head again, still smiling. 'Amazing,' he said.

Mab groaned. 'Enough already. We should lock you both in a box and you can talk about this stuff together where nobody else can hear you.'

'I wouldn't mind,' France said, and I tried not to like that too much. I concentrated on not changing colour.

Mab crouched down and said to Knox, 'Don't listen to them – listen to me. I can actually take you time-travelling.'

Knox looked at me for confirmation. 'Can she?'

'Your big sister and my big brother just talk about it,' she told him. 'But I can actually do it. Right there in that kitchen. Want to come?'

'When?' he said.

'How about now?'

He held out his hand to me. His feet were dancing, like he couldn't wait to go. 'Elk. Will you come too?'

France filmed us on his phone. I have watched it a thousand times over. Us in the Before. Standing in the kitchen with our backs to the sinks and the fridges to our right, two of them, the massive kind with double doors and an ice dispenser and a freezer down the whole of one side. They look like space-age sarcophagi, like you wouldn't be surprised to open them and find Walt Disney and the Queen of England there in cryonic suspension, waiting for another spin of the wheel. We are small next to them, Mab and I, with Knox in the middle. We all have so much growing still to do.

Mab starts jumping backwards and forwards in front of them. The floor is black and shiny, beetle's back, deep space, oil slick. Less than a metre, probably, from point to point, but she takes each jump like she is leaping over an infinite chasm, all preparation and peril.

'Copy me,' she says. 'Do what I'm doing,' so we start jumping about beside her. The look on our faces is such a mix of things – super-focused and silly and dare-devil wild, just leaping around in Mab's kitchen.

Our earlier selves. Our outfits. The way I tried to force my hair to part on the wrong side. It's not even two years ago, but we were in those bodies, the same bodies. My shirt was me-sized then, and now I'm not sure it would even fit.

'Am I doing it right,' Knox says, breathless. 'Is this it?' and I am bewildered really, and Mab is laughing and laughing, so delighted.

'Look at the CLOCKS,' she tells us, arms flinging round to point at those fridges, each with their digital display.

The camera zooms in so you can see it. One at 11:17; the other 13:23. You can hear France laughing.

'SEE?' Mab says. 'Time travel.'

Two hours and six minutes.

'It IS.' I'm laughing, and I look straight at France, at the camera.

Knox is like a lightning bolt in boy-form. 'OH. We ARE!'

The others look straight at the future then, at France and his phone, still jumping. Mab's screwed-up nose and my brother's apple cheeks. I am blowing the hair out of my face, lit up, squinting. We none of us have any idea of what's in store.

Stevie takes a tissue out of the box and blows her nose with it. She takes off her glasses and dabs at her eyes.

'Oh, Elk,' she says. 'What a terrible waste.'

Want to hear about my kind of time travel? Mab says, watching Stevie's tears with cool fascination.

'Yes,' I say. 'Tell me.'

She sighs. She is all grown up now. The Mab in that video is just a baby compared.

It looks like both of us walking out of those woods, alive.

11. CODE

France was two years above us in school and people liked him, staff and pupils, so we got a free pass from everyone, more or less. Thanks to him, nobody messed with his little sister and her sidekick best friend. Even if they didn't know our names, we were safe. It was tacit, as in unspoken. It just was. I spent my primary school years trying to be invisible around the powerful girls who didn't like me. But here, it was different. I learned pretty quickly that I could be myself and get away with it. I'm not sure anything inside a school building is worth more than that.

Mab said it was weird how many girls in his year

already knew who she was and tried so hard to be nice to her.

'I mean, I like it,' she said. 'Don't get me wrong. But it's just a bit obvious.'

'Obvious?' I said.

'Ulterior motives,' she told me, pulling this face. 'They flirt with him by sucking up to me.'

'Oh,' I said. Oddly disappointed.

'I know, right?' Mab was laughing. 'Disgusting but true.'

France was big, but he was quiet. He wasn't the kind of brother that threw stuff at you or burst in the room and jumped on your head. Mab said, 'I'd kill him if he tried it, that's why,' and she might have been right, but it wasn't that at all. He was just gentle. Kind. I never once saw him throw his weight around. I remember he caught a cat once that was lost and crying in the school playground. A half-grown kitten. He picked it up and held it like it was made of paper, made of glass, and it sat there in the palm of his hand, plate-eyed and blinking, scared out of its wits of everything except for him. I knew a person that soft couldn't hurt anyone. For a long time, I thought I was right.

Mum and Dad were either at work or neck-deep in baby Knox stuff, so I was with my gran quite a lot after school, and at Mab's, where I was always welcome. I couldn't decide which place I liked better – Gran's or Mab's or home. I was happiest in all of them.

'An abundance of riches,' Gran called it, and Mab said, 'You are properly, *properly* loved.'

It was a good time and I'm glad I actually noticed, because nothing lasts for ever. Everything passes and then gets gone.

Mab loved being at my house too. She liked my bedroom and the fact it looked out into a hundred windows so she could be nosy and see what other people were up to in their own houses. From her room you could only see birds and trees and sky. She liked the way Knox made a mess of the place, and was always building something or knocking it down. She liked his train track and his toy cars. She liked the way my dad talked about politics and the way my mum pretended not to agree with him. She liked the way Knox said goodnight to us from inside his bedroom and we answered him, our voices sounding all together in the hall.

Mab and France called their parents Joss and Jay. It didn't sound weird in their house, although mine would have had something to say if I was suddenly all, 'Hey, Jack and Alan.' Joss was painting us. Mab and me. We sat with our heads together on a seat in her studio, facing each other, whispering nonsense, spilling secrets. Well. Mab spilled her secrets to me. I couldn't tell her all of mine. I worried she might laugh at me, and I took things much too seriously for that.

'When will it be finished?' I asked Joss, when the smell of Jay's cooking called us downstairs to eat. She moved a strand of my hair over my shoulder with her jasmine hands and said, 'Never. There will always be changes. I want to paint the pair of you all of the time.'

I told France that my gran was a physicist. I told him I wanted to study it like she did and he lent his books to me, let me sit in his room once or twice and listen to these lectures, quantum physics at Caltech in the 1960s. The professor's name was Richard Feynman. France said he was famous, a legend, and he was a very good talker. Funny as well as mind-bendingly smart. I didn't understand most of what he was talking about, but France said that didn't matter because it was all about the wonder to start with. That's what drew you in.

'Even the experts don't get it,' he told me, 'because it doesn't really make any sense.'

'*You* don't make any sense,' Mab said, hanging in the doorway. 'Stop trying to steal my best friend away from me with your weird incomprehensible science talks.'

She was smiling, but she meant it. I'd get up and leave his room. And every time, I wanted to leave it less and less.

Gran's illness was known as progressive, which means it went steadily downhill and there was nothing we could do to stop it. I don't know how ready Mum and Dad were for it, but it definitely crept up on me a bit. I just thought she was forgetful or distracted, until the downhill suddenly got so she was falling off a cliff.

Year nine, and the afternoons were getting dark. I've always liked that. I was doing homework at her little kitchen table and the radio was on. She was singing some old-time tunes in a voice like a doll trapped underwater. My head was full of maths. Factors and multiples. She was making us her pasta with drunk tomato sauce. It had a bit of vodka in it to make the tomatoes sweeter. She must have done it about a hundred times before. She was bringing the pan full of boiling hot water from the hob to the sink to drain it and she stopped in the middle of the room, steam rising, and stared at me.

'How long have you been back?' she said.

I laughed. I thought she was joking. 'Since three thirty.'

'Was it a long flight?'

I glanced up at her and she had this look on her face. Different. Hard and closed up. Like I didn't even know her.

'Flight?' I said, and we stared at each other for like a beat, before the lights in her face came back on and she was my gran again and her mouth made the shape of an O and she dropped the boiling water all down her own legs.

I remember her shins went scarlet and her face went white. I remember she sat down in a chair and she was shivering and making a kind of cooing noise like a terrified dove. I didn't want to touch her because I knew it would only make it worse. She was telling me not to call the doctor because she'd be in trouble, or something like that.

She said, 'I thought you were my sister.' She said, 'If you tell them, they'll just take me away.' She was babbling a bit. I didn't even know she had a sister. I figured she was in shock. I phoned home, but there was no answer. Dad's mobile was off and Mum wasn't picking up. So I phoned Mab's house and her dad said, 'Hello, Jay speaking.'

I think the first word I said to him was, 'Help.'

I had to tell him how to get to Gran's flats. He was there in less than ten minutes with France in the front seat. Together they helped get her in the car. She was crying quite a lot at that point. She must have been in so much pain. I sat in the back with her and held her hand and I remember how old it was, all knuckled and twisted, like a bird's claw. France watched us over his shoulder, but he didn't say anything. I don't think anybody spoke.

A&E was carnage. In our row there was a man with a nail through his thumb and a woman who couldn't stop throwing up in a bucket, even though she had nothing left to lose. A glassy-eyed baby whose parents looked like they were losing their minds, and a couple of kids who had come off their bikes while they were playing chicken on the cliffs. Nobody was having a good time and the nurses were running around like worker ants and the lady on reception wasn't taking any trouble from anyone, which seemed fair enough, given the scene. Jay left, because he had work stuff he couldn't get out of, but my dad was on his way, and France stayed with me. Gran was shivering by then like you wouldn't believe and France took off his jacket and wrapped it round her. I stroked her hair and I whispered, 'It's okay,' over and over again, and she said to me in a small voice, 'I want my mum.'

France saw my face then and he took my hand too. He just squeezed it and we sat there, a girl and a boy and an old lady, hand in hand like one of those cutout chains of paper people, dancing across a room. We were still sitting like that when my dad came in. I watched him hide everything he must have been thinking behind this mask, this placid smile, a shipwreck at the bottom of a lake. Gran looked at him like he was a stranger when he said, 'Oh, Mum, look at the state of you. What on earth have you done?'

'Where's Mab?' I said to France then, while Dad put his arms round Gran and held her. It was the first moment I'd thought to ask.

'Out with Joss,' he said. 'Swimming, I think. Shopping.'

One of his hands was still in mine and the other was on his own knee, fingers drumming. He was looking at the ground. France has a good profile. Strong nose, full mouth. I watched him. I took my time and took him in.

'Thank you for coming,' I said. 'It was really kind of you to do that.'

He let go of my hand then. 'I'd do anything for you, Elk,' he said, soft and quiet, and then he looked at me, and something happened. I don't know. The same but different. Something wordless was said. I was on the outside of it and then I wasn't. Like a bank vault, with the code keyed in and all the locked doors between us opening one by one.

12. RIBBON

I tried on too many of Mab's clothes before the party.
I'm sorry now that I wasted the little time we had left
just getting dressed. I felt like a cheap version of her
in everything.

'Try this one,' she said. 'And this one. The black
one. You'll look amazing in that.'

I didn't want to look amazing in anything. I
wanted to change my mind and stay in and drink
tea, maybe watch a good film. I wanted to put my
sweatpants back on.

'Resist the urge,' Mab told me, her face up close
while she did my mascara. Her throat when she swallowed. The tiny chicken pox scar on her neck.

I resisted, and we went downstairs to where France was eating leftovers in the kitchen.

'You look good,' he said, and Mab said, 'Shut up,' and when I said, 'Thank you,' every cell in my body tried not to reach for him, tried not to blush.

He drove us to Freya Fisher's house on the far edge of town. Stuck on its own like someone dropped it and hadn't gone back again to pick it up. That ribbon of road through the trees and out again. No street lights. No cameras. No proof. He had to park round the corner because there were so many cars in the yard. We could hear the party ahead of us, the sound system, bass, and the buzz of people, a hundred voices yelling over each other, all talking at once. I whistled slowly. Mab raised an eyebrow.

'Freya Fisher's thrown a *party*,' she said, and the surprise in her voice made us laugh.

There was this pull to it, this high feeling in the air, excited, magnetic. Loud. So loud I could still hear it later, the same way light leaves an impression on your retina and makes nagging shapes of itself in the dark.

'Are you coming?' I said to France, and he shook his head.

'I don't think so.'

'Oh go on,' Mab said. 'Just for a bit. Freya Fisher will be so honoured she'll probably cry.'

France laughed and switched the engine off and we sat there while the water pummelled the windows, lights flashing, on and off, through the trees.

'One, two, three,' I said, and we all got out of the car.

The rain was falling in sheets, I swear, like the sky just had buckets.

'Whose idea was this anyway?' Mab said, and she stuck her tongue out at me from under the hood of her coat. Every time I turned to look at her, I got a faceful of wet. So I didn't look at her, because I didn't know there were so few chances to look at her left.

The whole yard was strung with lights when we rounded the corner, the bounce and glow of it, the silhouettes of arms and heads and legs all tangled, all moving like one creature to the same beat, all breaking apart and gathering again. Mab took my hand and we ran and dived into the middle of it, leaving France somewhere behind. Everyone was there, and so happy to see each other and so relieved that school was over and life was about to begin.

Someone said, 'Is that your brother?' and someone else called out, 'FRANCE!'

'Was I right or was I right?' Mab shouted over the noise of everything.

'You're always right,' I shouted back.

I don't know how much later it was when we were standing in the upstairs hallway, in line for the bathroom, me and Mab. France was in the garden with the wolf pack, our name for the alpha-male crowd from school. I don't know what the collective noun for budding misogynists is – an entitlement, maybe – but anyway, the wolf pack would do. Our bathroom line shuffled forward slowly, groups of girls in twos and threes. There were these old pictures of Freya Fisher and her sisters behind Mab's head, all in matching dresses, looking like they grew up in a cult.

She said, 'How can you not like a girl with a childhood like that?'

I said I'd like her better if the dresses matched the curtains, and she said, 'I couldn't like you better if I tried.'

'Where's your brother?' a drunk girl in front of us said.

'Yeah, the hot one,' chipped in her friend.

'Outside,' Mab said. 'Playing with wolves.'

They frowned at her. 'Is he seeing anyone?' the first one said.

I tried not to hate them.

Mab smiled sweetly. 'Don't think so,' she said. 'Why don't you go and ask him yourself.'

When we got our turn in the bathroom, she fixed her eyeliner, saw to mine. There were beers in the bathtub and Freya Fisher had pinned a note to the wall in her perfect bubble writing that said, press twice to flush.

'Looking good,' Mab said to us both in the mirror, and she got her phone out and took the last ever pictures of us, barking prompts like a fashion photographer. 'Corn-fed. Hard-up. Vulnerable. Fierce.'

She said, 'If you laugh like that, your make-up will run,' and I told her, 'I laugh the way I laugh. I can't help it.'

She was looking at her own reflection when she said it. 'What would I do without you, Elk.' I said, 'You'll never have to know,' and then the girls still waiting to use the bathroom started banging on the door.

'You like him though, don't you,' she said, all

casual like she wasn't saying anything much.

'Who?' I said.

'My brother, stupid.'

'Oh,' I said, and I should have told her then. *Yes. I do. More than like.* I should have told her what had finally started to happen with me and France, only a few weeks before. I could have got it over with and been honest. I wish I had.

But, 'No more than I did yesterday,' was all I said because I figured it wasn't lying and it wasn't the whole truth. I'm a coward, when it comes down to it. I guess I failed that particular test.

'Would you be with him?' Mab said, staring at me in the mirror, pinning me down.

'Why are you asking?' I said.

She smoothed her hair. Her eyes flicked away. 'There's an atmosphere.'

My pulse was like a hammer, like nought to sixty. 'Really? I hadn't noticed.'

Mab laughed. 'You wouldn't, Elk. You never did.'

I took that as a compliment, and then she said, 'He really likes you,' and I didn't mean to look so happy about it, but the smile just kind of hijacked my whole face.

Mab didn't smile back. There was something flinty about her. Her frown was sharp.

'Just so you know,' she said. 'I wouldn't like it.'

'Wow,' I said. 'OK.'

I was there in the bathroom and I was also like a drone of myself, flying up high, watching from above. I was two people at once, feeling two conflicting things about the idea of me and France.

Why can't we? And at the same time, How could we?

The whole damn universe is inconsistent and contradicts itself. Why shouldn't I contradict myself too?

'Sorry,' Mab said. 'I'm just being honest. You know, getting out in front of it or whatever.'

'Sure,' I said. 'I appreciate that,' but truthfully I didn't. I wanted to leave the bathroom. I wanted Mab to stop telling me what to do.

'Elk . . .' She held on to my hand. 'I'd hate it.'

'Let's go,' I said, and she said, 'Okay,' and let go again as I went ahead of her down the hallway.

'Can I remind you of the downsides?' Mab said.

'Of what?'

'Of France.'

'If you want,' I told her, hardly listening.

'I won't hold back though.'

I laughed at her. 'When did you ever?'

'He eats like a pig,' she said.

'I've seen him.'

'He snores.'

'I know. You can hear him from your room.'

'His feet are ugly.'

'Are they? I hadn't noticed.'

'He's kind of arrogant. And he broke my scooter when I was eight.'

'He's not arrogant,' I said.

'Elk. My scooter.'

I laughed. 'He told me it was on its last legs.'

'Yeah, well he finished it off,' she said. 'He killed it.'

'Are you finished?' I said. 'Is that it?'

'It's not funny,' Mab said. 'I'm not joking. It would be too weird. Please don't do anything.'

'We won't,' I said, but saying it was already a lie.

In the chaos of the kitchen, she poured us some shots that tasted like green sweets and ethanol. We shook hands like a contract, clinked cups.

'Do you promise?' she asked me.

I didn't answer.

'Do you swear on your life?'

I picked up the bottle. 'Shall we risk another one?'

She pulled a face. 'It's so gross.'

'Once more, no more,' I told her, which was a thing that Knox used to say.

'Done,' she said. 'Are you annoyed?'

'Me?' I said. 'No.'

'I just love you,' she said. 'I don't want to lose you.'

'You can't lose me. You found me,' I said.

13. STATUE

Knox's favourite thing to climb, once he got good at it, was a larger-than-life marble statue of a woman in the square outside the town hall. She wore a hooded cape, and held a sheaf of papers in one hand and what looked like a long, sharp compass in the other. Head-to-toe bird filth and other droppings, kind of stinking, she stood there all stoic and unseeing, sometimes with a traffic cone on her head. Her name was Mary something and, in the nature of things, she was there because she was somebody's wife or somebody's sister. I liked her. Her clothing draped like silk rather than stone, the folds of her cloak ramped like steps right up to the top. The details of her face had reached a kind of blandness, like the fibreglass fisherman in the yellow hat that used to stand outside the fish and chip shop on the pier, until his nose fell off and people started putting their cigarettes out in the space.

We used to call her Poor Mary. Like, 'I'll meet you by Poor Mary at six.'

Knox climbed her mostly because he wanted to climb everything. A kind of world navigation, same as when he learned to talk and staggered around naming everything to himself – pepper, ladder, table, juice. Like a bee. Hungry. Mapping the world.

Mab and I were in charge of him that day. The three of us were just taking our time and wandering around, following Knox's timetable, which was this mix of intense detail and total lack of end goal.

'I love being with your brother,' Mab said. 'There is literally no knowing what's going to happen next.'

People looked on disapprovingly when we let him climb Poor Mary. One old lady tutted. Mum would have told him to get down, I'm sure of it, but he was good at it and safe enough, and he really loved the view.

'Pretty high, hey,' Mab said when people glared at us, and they arranged their faces and looked for something else to judge.

Poor Mary's plinth was grimy, and her name-plate was greened the way old copper goes, quite beautifully, and the letters were all laced with gunk, like the stuff that lives between floorboards. Somebody had stuck gum on it. People had written things, *ROSE LOVES CRACK AND EAT THE RICH AND CLEAN ME 07/05.*

Knox reached up to grab onto her ankle, and in less than a minute he had scaled the steps of her stone cape and was sitting on her shoulders. That boy really could climb. I looked up at his face with the sun flickering down through the leaves and the traffic slowing to a halt on the corner. She didn't move. Not even the dance of the light changed her. She stayed exactly the same.

Mab was going at the stuck bits of gum with her door key. Trying to prise them off. She was frowning. 'Why do people do this?' she said. 'It's so completely wrong.'

Knox caught a butterfly. A red admiral. They were everywhere in the summer. I kept finding them pressed up against windows and wilting on the carpet. I kept letting them out.

'Look at this,' he said, and he beamed down at

us. It opened and closed like a slow clap on his outstretched palm.

'It's because you're salty,' Mab said.

'Am I?'

'Yeah. Sweaty. They like it,' she said.

Knox stayed still so he didn't disturb it, and he watched it up close.

My gran used to say a red admiral was good luck. A message from the departed, she called them. Just quickly saying hello. I imagined it was her for a second, dipping down to see how Knox was growing up. He didn't remember her the same way I did. They weren't nearly as close. He was so little when she started forgetting. They just didn't have enough time.

We were meeting France at the beach. I was looking forward to seeing him a whole lot more than I should. I didn't know what was going on between us right then; I just knew that it was something. It had been growing all this time, underground, out of sight, and now it was starting to come up, the way green shoots just appear out of nowhere in the spring. It had that same kind of hopefulness about it, for me.

When we got there it was late, around four, and pretty busy. Mab waved at a few people, went to chat to some others. Knox headed straight for the water and I kept my eye on him and tried to watch for France at the same time. The sea frilled like lace around my ankles. Frothed and fussed and then shushed itself away. Soon the warmth of the day was nearly over. Clouds settled in and the change in the light went from gradual to sudden.

Mab came over and nudged me with her wet foot. 'Why is my brother always late?'

'Is he?' I said, pretending it didn't matter to me one way or the other.

'Maybe he's not coming,' she said. 'That would be just like him.'

I nodded, playing along. 'Yeah, maybe he forgot.'

I made my peace with it. Soon the tide would come and smooth things over. Tomorrow was another day. There are terrible things going on in the world, every second, and we all know a quick disappointment on a beach isn't one of them.

'His loss,' Mab said.

'I guess so.'

'It will be when I kill him.'

I laughed. 'All right, queen of drama. No need for you to do that.'

It was the hour of the day when the sea and the sky are the same colour and that colour is nothing, so it's like you are living on some outpost at the edge of the world. Knox was throwing himself around in the breakers, an invisible force dragging him under and spitting him back out, wave-drenched, arms flailing, hands outstretched like flat little stars. His grin was shark's teeth, his eyes were rolling. The waves were chucking him about like an empty burger box and he was noisy, squealing, loving it.

Mab pointed to France, running along the waterline towards us. 'Here he is,' she said. 'Saving his own life.'

'Sorry,' he said.

'It's fine,' I told him. 'We haven't been here very long.'

Mab stared at me, all wide-eyed, and then at him. 'We have, actually,' she said. 'You're really late.'

He bent down, propped his hands on his thighs. 'Sorry,' he said again. 'I really ran.'

'Your nose is bleeding,' she said, and he caught it with the back of his hand, searched in his pockets for something to use. The wind bit and needled, sharp with sand, I guess, singing. His shirt was black with pearl buttons. They glinted when they caught the light.

My brother, by the way, thinks France is the stuff of legend. Like someone out of a storybook. Doesn't matter how often he sees him, it is like awestruck kid meets a giant. He watched France the same way you'd watch the big yachts loom like tower blocks into the bay – with envy and wonder and suspicion. Knox believed in giants, fully. Giants and ogres and trolls. They were as real to him as marsh-grass and snowflakes. As Saturn and Greenland. As gravity and our very own mum. He was lying on his belly at the start of the water, very still, his face half-under, ears like sea caves, eyes burning, waiting for France to notice him back.

France picked up a cuttlebone, brushed off the sand. He was wearing a ring made from a spoon, bashed flat and curled around itself like a sleeping animal. You can start out as one thing and end up another, I guess. There is a way. People think it's a shell, the cuttlebone, but it's this buoyant internal organ, incredibly clever, chalky and lightweight, like the floats you use when you're learning to swim. The beach is littered with them most days. You can buy them ground to powder, to feed to your pets.

'Come out of the water, fish boy,' Mab said. 'Come and say hello.'

Knox got to his feet and padded over, squinting up at France, his free hand shielding his eyes from the sky. I watched what he was watching. Tried to see what he could see. France's hands were a state. Great cuts of meat with knuckles like battlements and raw, scarred palms. I pictured hot ropes rushing through them, holding on for dear life. Knox saw them too. I watched his pupils open like portals. More questions flooding out.

'What happened to you?' he said.

France closed his hands up into fists. 'Occupational hazard,' he said, and Knox didn't stop staring, the way kids just don't. He was standing on one leg now like a scrawny flamingo in the salt flats. He was shivering and Mab covered his shoulders with a towel.

'What does that mean?'

'Like a danger that comes with the job,' I said.

'Like King Harold?'

Mab laughed, and I said, 'Kind of, okay, yes.'

Knox was into the Bayeux Tapestry and King Harold was his favourite. He drew pictures and pictures of this tiny man harpooned through the face, and drops of blood like soldier ants, marching and marching. He couldn't stop looking. He wanted to know if this giant had ever gone into battle. If he'd ever skewered a king right in the eye. I could tell by his face. Pure wonder.

'What kind of job?' he said.

'I was working in our garden,' France told him.

'My brother likes to wrestle the trees in our garden,' Mab said, smiling.

'Big ones,' France said. 'Sometimes they bite.'

'I'm going to be five,' Knox said, because that was impressive, at least to him. He told a lot of people how old he was going to be. Random shoppers, people on buses. It seemed important. Like getting to five would be something good he'd done by himself, without any help.

France bent down low to the ground and Knox drew the number with his finger, fallen over, like the five had passed out right there at his feet.

Their heads were almost touching. Amber and sand.

Knox smiled.

'Oh look,' France said, surprise in his voice, and we watched the bone start to jump about on his palm like it had a life of its own, like it wanted nothing more than to get back in the water and swim.

'What's it doing?' said Knox, and he peered into the bowl of France's hands, the way he would look deep into a cage at a mouse or a snake or a rabbit. The cuttlebone jumped up and touched him on the nose.

'It kissed me!' Knox said, delight flooding his pencil arms, his twig fingers, his puffball knees.

'Have you ever seen little turtles hatch out of their eggs?' France said, and Knox shook his head.

France crouched down low, still a lot taller than Knox. He looked like a solitary rock.

'The eggs are buried in the sand,' he said. 'To protect them from predators, and the weather.'

He pushed the cuttlebone in deep, his arm like the root of a tree. Knox's lips were dry and salty. His eyes shone. Less than a metre from our feet, the sand started to quiver.

'Then, when they're ready, they climb out,' France said, only looking at Knox, who was watching the cuttlebone break the surface now with its blind nose, claw its way up, full of purpose, full of something like life, although it couldn't be, although we all knew what it was. Just a dead piece of fish and nothing else.

Even Mab followed its newborn, trembling line down the sand towards the water.

'They know what to do,' France was saying. 'They know, long before they begin. It's built in. Instinctive. It is thousands of years of knowing.'

'Thousands?' Knox repeated in a whisper.

'They swim,' France said, reaching the shoreline and not stopping, just walking in, while the cuttlebone dipped and splashed with the spirit he'd given it. 'I have followed them out as far as I could go, and they just keep swimming.'

'You've seen them?' Knox's face was lit up. 'In real life?'

More cuttlebones rose to the surface then, joined the first one, floating in formation on the skin of the sea. France's pockets must have been full of them. It was the only explanation I could think of, but Knox didn't need one. He was in the presence of magic. He turned in a circle, wide-eyed and awestruck.

'They start like this,' France said, 'like little seeds. And they get so big.'

'How big? As big as Elk?' Knox said, and France's eyes narrowed.

'Bigger.'

'No way,' said Knox.

'Ten times heavier than Elk and Mab put together. Forty times heavier than you. And a hundred years old.'

'Where do they go?'

'They swim for thousands of miles. But they always come back to the place they were born, and lay more eggs, and the hatching starts again.'

The water was up to Knox's waist. He was beaming. He looked at me. 'I love this story.'

'It's not a story, Knox,' Mab told him. 'My brother knows stuff. It's a hundred per cent true.'

He had this smile on his face like you wouldn't believe. He brought us a crab. A tiny thing, one claw sluggish, legs mid-air, still running.

'Look at this,' he said, and he beamed at France first, then at me; then he dropped it into France's palm. 'It's for you.'

'Thank you,' France said.

'But put it back,' Knox said. 'Let it go, or Elk will tell you off.'

'She will?' France was smiling, but Knox was serious. He put his hands behind his back like an umpire at the cricket, stuck his bottom jaw out. 'She really will.'

France took his sweatshirt off.

'You look like the one in Market Street,' Knox said.

'The what?'

'The one with no top on. The big one.'

'Statue,' Mab told him, laughing.

'Oh,' he said. 'Thank you. I think.'

Knox turned back and forth at the waist like a pepper grinder. 'You're welcome.'

When the sun was almost gone and the beach was dark grey in the shadows and emptying, we started walking, back the way France had run, along the edge of the water. Mab and Knox were ahead of us. She held his hand, and he took two steps to her one, and they were talking and talking, same as usual. France was so close I couldn't have fit a piece of paper between us, but we weren't touching, not then. Not quite yet. The tide was on its way out, so our footprints vanished behind us, almost instantly. The sun was low, leaving, almost gone. Mab's favourite time to walk it After, so she can pretend that we are ghosts together, not just her, on her own. She runs along facing backwards, excited, shouting, *Look! Where are you? Elk! Where the hell have you gone?*

14. FIREWORK

Two weeks before the party, I called France greedy. That's how it finally started. I didn't say the word for nothing, and he didn't take it personally. A seagull ate his sock and that's the truth right there, the seed of the new me and France tree.

I could wish for a sweeter word, like *honey*. A clearer one, like *sky*. But no. I called him greedy. There's no changing a single thing that happened, not for any of us, and so there's no changing that.

Mab was working at the cafe and I'd been killing time without her at the beach. The sand was warm. I read my book without reading it, checked my phone for no reason, drank some water, zoned out on the sea. I lay back and shut my eyes, spent a while trying to find a word for the colour I could see through my own skin. The buttons of my dress lined up, cold dots from throat to hip, my wrists and shins felt exposed. It was non-specifically noisy. I must have looked like I was sleeping, but I could not have been more awake. I was that thing in the poem. The still point of the turning world. Whatever. Somewhere there is always a clock ticking. When I sat up, there he was, stretched out on the sand between me and the water, this familiar mountain range of a boy, dressed in black like a stagehand, all quiet and no colour. I knew he was leaving for university at the end of the summer, but here he was, acres of him, shoes off, still and solid as rock, like moving wasn't possible. Like he could never really be gone. His eyes were closed and he looked peaceful. All by himself, in the best possible way.

I would have left him alone if it wasn't for the seagull, which was young as well as foolish. Not fridge-white yet, more fog-grey, feathers like the inside of a wet cloud. Not cruel-faced yet either, but almost. On its way, clearly. The seagull code is harsh. Act first, think later – eat/regret eat/regret/ eat/

regret. I watched it stalk up behind him and fish the sock right out of his shoe. It had it speared and swallowed almost before he noticed. I saw it all happen, while France just caught the toe-end disappearing last into its gullet like a black wool tongue, the bird all-over fritzing with doubt and panic.

He made a quick, sharp noise without words, sat up like someone from a bad dream. The bird stared him out. Eyes like buttons, body jerking, pure denial and a kind of wild shame coming off it.

'What?' he asked it, reaching for his things, and his voice was softer than you'd expect with all that going on. I thought he would boom at it like Goliath, but he just didn't. He was gathering his stuff around him. 'You want the other one now? You can't have it. It's mine.'

That's when I said it. 'Greedy.'

I didn't know I was going to say it until I had. Split-second decisions cast long shadows, spread their wings wide like albatross, and the world turns away and keeps turning.

He turned and smiled at me. He was holding the widowed sock in his hand.

'Unbelievable.'

I remember the roll of the water, behind him all the sound of the sea, and then he said, 'Elk,' like he was glad about it. Like he was pleased it was me.

'Hi,' I said.

'How long have you been sitting there?'

'Not long.'

'I'll miss it,' he said.

'Miss what?'

I felt the beam of his gaze, the pylon hum of his attention.

'This beach,' he said. 'The mad birds.' He looked me straight in the eye. 'Home.'

The gull was fleeing the scene, stuffed to the gills, half-running, half-flying, kind of messy and frantic, and he stood up to watch it go.

The beach was loud and crowded, full summer, but we made our own small quietness there near the edge of the water. There was a smile rising in me like a bubble.

'So,' he said. 'What happens now?'

He looked at his watch. Old-fashioned. The kind you wound by shaking it.

'You sit there,' I said. 'Guard your other sock.'

France's laugh was always a prize. Out and then

done, loud and quick like a firework. As soon as he finished, you wanted to win it again. 'I meant for the bird.'

I shrugged. 'You know it will have eaten worse.'

'Still,' he said, watching me. 'I'll worry.'

I couldn't think when I'd last seen him without Mab. Little waves came in and got dragged back out. I looked away before he did, drew a curve in the sand with my foot, an unclosed bracket that would sit there unfinished until the sea chose to take it away. He smiled down at it, my started sentence. I liked being near him. I guess I always have.

'Where's my sister?' he said.

'Work.'

'Making bad coffee.'

I laughed. She really wasn't very good at it. 'Yeah. Arguing about the definition of a flat white.'

'She's cross with me,' he said.

'Why? What have you broken this time?'

He smiled. 'Nothing.'

'What then?'

He threw a stone into the water. 'It doesn't matter,' he said.

A gang of kids was throwing a neon ball around.

The sound of their voices cut in sharply, like the volume had been turned up.

'Are you ready for university?' I asked him.

'Not yet. I don't think so.'

'I guess there's a lot to do,' I said. 'Before you go. A lot to think about.'

He was looking at his hands when he said, 'Will you miss me?'

'Me?' I said.

'Yes, Elk. You.'

'Oh, you know,' I said.

He smiled. 'No,' he said. 'I don't.'

I didn't know how honest I could be. Mab was my best friend in the world, but France had been a constant too. Always there when I went over. Always on my mind, one way or another. Maybe it was time.

'Yes,' I said. 'Of course I'll miss you.'

'Really?' he said.

It felt good to tell him. 'Yes, France. I will.'

'Thank you,' he said. 'That means a lot.'

I put my hands in my pockets. 'You're welcome,' I said.

He laughed a little. 'That's why my sister's cross.'

★

124

I went to get us an ice cream. I needed the distraction. I think I needed to move away from him for a minute. I had this kind of vertigo.

Halfway up the beach, the wolf pack pounced. Masters of their own tiny universe, beelining it over to me across the sand's lunar surface, like God's collective gift. They looked good. They always looked good, like a boy band, 24 carat, but that's no substitute for decency or a personality, let's face it. Mab used to say she wouldn't mind waking up as one of those boys one morning, just for a day, so she could fully understand how it felt. Still, my guess was it was tumbleweed in there. Tumbleweed and something darker, some insidious form of help-yourself.

'Elena,' the front one said. I think his name was Tom, but they were all interchangeable to me. 'How you doing?'

'Fine thanks,' I said. 'Good.'

'All on your own?'

'Well,' I said, looking at the packed shoreline. 'Hardly.'

I went round them, but they moved as one, like a pack like a swarm like a shadow, surrounding me, walked with me like we were going somewhere

125

together, I guess because they'd decided that's how it would be. Reality existed for those boys because they let it. Imagine that, feeling like you can run your own world, and getting away with it.

'Where's your friend?' one of them said, and another said, 'Mab,' all confidence and dazzle, like sharp knives.

'Work,' I said.

'Nice dress,' one of them said, grabbing at me with his fingers. He lifted his hand so the hem went up over my knees. I slapped him down.

'Don't do that,' I said, and he laughed, quietly and kind of *at* me, and I turned my face away then because I was furious, and not about to let them enjoy that too.

It wasn't a new thing. It's how they were in school with everyone. Casually predatory. We know not to get left alone with them, not to get cornered, like it's our responsibility to stay safe, not theirs to be something other than dangerous. Our word against theirs, and almost always our fault somehow, until the world changes, and we are none of us holding our breath.

When I saw France walking towards us, I stepped away from them, closer to him. Pulled one of their hands off my wrist.

126

'You good?' France asked me.

'I'm fine.'

They looked at each other. 'All right?' he said. Not friendly, just barely polite, and I watched them shrink from him instantly, their swank and bravado wilting, fizzling out. They backed off, turned away. He made it look that easy.

'Are you sure?' he said.

I nodded. 'I'm used to it.'

He hadn't stopped watching them. 'What a world. I'm sorry I noticed so late.'

'Your timing was perfect,' I told him. 'Let's just leave it at that.'

In her last dreamlike days, my gran would stare at things and speak their colours. A tray she liked was called 'green' and her bed was 'the pink and white'. She would have looked at France's eyes and chosen petrol and wine-dark, shadows and cave-mouth, evening, air-force, mahogany. He was – he is – a very beautiful boy.

I bought him his ice cream. I insisted, in fact. 'For rescuing me and everything,' I said, and he knew I was only half-serious. He pulled this hero face.

I was supposed to be meeting Mab from work. She was only doing a half day.

'Don't go,' he said, and he spread his arms like wings, turned in a circle, part my best friend's big brother, part Angel of the North. 'Stay with me.'

I didn't answer straight away, so he said, 'Remember that today a bird robbed me. I could do with some good luck.'

'And the good luck would be what?'

'I told you.'

I said, 'But she's waiting for me.'

'Message her.'

'I'm not doing that,' I said.

He took my hand for a second. I watched him do it. I watched our fingers intertwine.

'I feel like we shouldn't be doing this,' I said.

He didn't look at me. 'That's what Mab says.'

'And what do you say?'

'I say you can't stop the sea.'

I felt all his bravery at once, all his shyness then, on my own skin. It really threw me.

'This has been a long time coming,' he said, and I said, 'Yes. It has. I agree.'

'We could argue about when it started.'

'A&E?' I asked him, and he touched my cheek when he said, 'Maybe before,' and I said, 'That's when it started for me.'

A cloud swept over the sun, small and quick.

'Can I come with you then?' France said. 'To meet Mab.'

'She won't like it.'

'She doesn't have to.'

'Nothing can happen, France,' I said.

'Sure,' he said. 'But what if it already has?'

He grinned at me, stood and swung his bag up and onto his back, the cable tendons in his neck, the dips and hollows of his shoulders like pools in the smooth rock. The boy is a pillar. The boy is a tall tree. I will never not think of him like that.

'Another reason to like you,' he told me.

'What? Because I'm loyal to your sister?'

'You're a good friend,' he said.

'I really love her.'

'I know you do.'

The horizon pulsed with light. We both watched it.

'Still,' he said. 'I was glad to finally get you to myself.'

'Finally what?'

'You heard me,' he said.

I did.

We were going to be late. Mab would be waiting. We started walking together up the beach. Three socks. Four trainers. Two beating hearts. I remember the exact and particular colour of the day.

He took my hand again.

Jesus God, I said to myself. *Holy crap.*

Then I turned away from him to hide my smile, to face the sun, to face the sea.

15. LIGHT

Freya Fisher's party turned out to be the kind of night where everything was working, a run of green lights and things just slotting so neatly into place. Perfect somehow, until it wasn't. The music was loud enough and good enough and there were beers and cheap fizzy wine and strong, sticky punch in little cups. Some people peaked too early, a few of them lost the plot, but there was also this great feeling everywhere, and all of us thinking about what was possible, what was going to happen next. It was hot in there. Everyone had this shine to them. Everyone was glowing.

I hadn't seen France since we left him in the front

yard. I thought he must be long gone. At some point, I went through the doors that said Don't Use Please into the garden to get some air. It had stopped raining and someone had lit a fire on the other side of the building. It was flinging these wild shapes across the roof. The air smelled like butterscotch and barbecue. Through the windows I could see Mab looking for me inside, working her way through the room in that dress. She had this way of making everyone feel good about something, making everybody smile. I remember her own smile when she saw me, how she pulled this face and waggled her fingers, her in the noise of the party, me outside in the quiet.

An hour later, we were both outside and I showed her Betelgeuse, which had started glowing unusually bright in the sky. I'd been reading about it in the paper. A star behaving strangely and apparently nobody could say why.

'It's dying, apparently,' I said. 'And when it finally goes, it'll be so bright you'll be able to see it in the daylight. It will make shadows, a bit like the sun.'

'When?' Mab said. 'Soon?' and I told her, 'More like thousands of years from now.'

Mab laughed. 'The stuff you are into requires too

132

much patience. All that planetary time or deep time or whatever you call it.'

'I'm a patient person,' I told her. 'What can I say?'

Someone was singing and somebody laughed; somebody whistled, loud, through their teeth. I could hear a dog barking in the distance. A good place for a party. No neighbours, no witnesses. Remote.

I said that *Betelgeuse* came from an Arabic word that means 'giant's shoulder'.

'Who told you that?' she said.

'My gran.'

We were standing there, staring up, and Mab was smiling. She put her arm around me, and I'm just so glad she did.

I said, 'The light we're seeing now is about six hundred years old, so the star could be dead already, and the news hasn't reached us.'

'Waiting down here,' she said. 'None the wiser. Always the last to know.'

16. IF

If I close my eyes, I can see her standing there in the black night with the stars in her eyes.

Or us walking down the high street, one earphone each, listening to this podcast she was crazy about, Rosa Luxemburg first, and then something about the theory of a feminist state. Apparently, we needed to educate ourselves. Times were changing, she said, and not fast enough. We had to walk close together to keep the earphones in our ears. I could feel Mab's part of the wire tugging as she moved away. At the corner of my eye, it looked like pulled gum.

I see her getting home with nothing on her mind but instant noodles.

See her standing on a dark road with her arms out to me, perfect and unbroken, before the end.

At the end of term. Days before. When she was out on the benches at lunchtime, ignoring the everyday drama and pretending to read the same book as me. This beginners' kind of tour of quantum physics that I'd been trying to tell her about for weeks. As soon as I finished it the first time, I went back to the beginning and started again.

'I'm still not done with it,' I told her. 'I might never actually stop.'

Mab's book was a hardback. I felt this flicker of envy and then I flattened it and got my own copy out of my pocket, dog-eared and shabby, a cheap copy, overdue at the library by more than a month.

'You're reading it,' I said, and she raised an eyebrow, and said, 'Well. I'm trying.'

'And?'

She dragged her eyes up from the page. Heavy lids, long lashes but real, not the baleen kind of add-ons half the girls in our year were wearing. Mab's eyes were a nice soft colour, with iron underneath. Like a curtain in front of a safe. '*Loving* it,' she said.

'Seriously?'

135

She nodded and went back to reading and when I asked her where she was up to, I watched her mark the word she was on with her whole face.

'Chapter four. "Entanglement". I think I'm reading this sentence for the thirteenth time.'

I was about to say something else. I opened my mouth to speak and then Mab slammed the book shut, hard, like dropping a piano lid.

'I can't lie to you,' she said.

'About what?'

'Anything.'

'Oh.'

'I *hate* it.'

I laughed. 'Really?'

'I haven't understood anything,' she said. 'Like literally not one thing.'

'That's fine,' I said. 'I don't understand it either. Not even the writer understands it and he's an expert.'

'That makes no sense.'

'Except it kind of does.'

'So, what, you rate him and everything, this expert who doesn't understand it.'

'Yes.'

She was smiling. 'And if you got a signed copy of the book, you'd be happy and stuff.'

'Oh my god,' I said. 'Imagine.'

Mab handed me her copy. 'Have mine.'

There was this drawing of an island on the front. Rocky and treeless. Just stuck there in a storm.

I started to say something, but Mab said, 'Shut up and open it.'

Somewhere on the school field, someone was getting their bag nicked and someone else was getting their heart broken and someone was telling a secret they had no right telling and someone was kicking a ball into someone else's face. And here I was, getting this gift for no reason, this signed hardback copy of my favourite book from Mab.

'Are you serious?' I said. 'Is this real?'

'France helped me, obviously,' she said. 'But yes. Happy Thursday, you geek.'

If I close my eyes, I can picture the time we went skinny-dipping in broad daylight. Early morning and the beach was pretty deserted, or I might never have done it. It wasn't long after my gran died. Mab's idea, and a kind of tribute, I suppose. Gran liked to swim without her clothes on. It used to wind my parents up, the nudist phase of her dementia. She never understood why they made such a fuss.

'Nothing wrong with it,' she said, 'it's just bodies,' and Dad busied himself with a plug socket inside a cupboard, and Mum said, 'Not in front of the kids, please, Mum,' like we didn't have bodies of our own.

I remember looking for somewhere to write her shopping down and I found a list in her shaky handwriting, the seven stages of getting naked in public, when she could remember the stages exactly, but not how to hold her own pen.

'Priorities,' I said at the time, and she said, 'Yes, Jackie.'

'I'm not Jackie. I'm Elk,' I said, 'Jackie's daughter,' and my gran said, 'Elk? What kind of name is that?'

She said it was a brilliant feeling, to be inside your own body instead of looking at it.

'Really?' I said.

She pointed her pen at the cupboard my dad was making himself scarce in. 'You should get your uptight husband to give it a try.'

'Gran,' I said. 'Gross. That's my dad.'

'No, Jack,' she said. 'Your dad was a natural. Ran

138

around like a kid without his pants on. Never laughed so much in his life.'

'Let's do it for her,' Mab said, because she knew I was struggling and I needed to do something. 'I've always wanted to,' she said. 'And you only live once and all that.'

Stage one, according to Gran: take your clothes off and lie on your stomach. That was easy enough.

Stage two: turn over and lie on your back, belly up. I felt vulnerable then, conspicuous. I figured any moment someone was going to notice. Mab was giggling.

'This is already a lot,' she said.

No one was looking. I was scanning the shoreline, keeping watch.

'Zero interest in us so far,' I said. 'Which is nice.'

Stage three: sit up. Which wasn't as bad as we thought. There was a breeze coming off the water and the sun was warm on our backs.

'I like it,' Mab said. 'I'm happy right here.'

Stage four: stand up. So we did. Mab watched me and laughed.

'You look like a meerkat,' she said, and she did an impression of me, which was bang on, and made us both cry with laughter. That's what gave us the strength for stage five, which was walking to the water.

'But like we mean it,' Mab said, styling it out. 'Like we might be enjoying ourselves.'

'We are,' I said. 'I am.'

'I know,' she said. 'Me too. Your clever gran.'

Something good was starting to happen. Not many chances a girl gets to be comfortable, in public, in her own skin. And here we were, occupying ourselves fully. It felt like a gift.

Stage six was the best part. Swim. The water held me up and it was cool but not cold and it dropped and swelled like it was breathing and we were part of it. I could taste the salt on my face from our laughing as well as the salt from the sea. Mab floated on her back, spouting water like a whale and then turned and went deep, the soles of her feet slick and shining.

When she came back up to the surface, she said, 'Are you ready?'

'For what?'

'Stage seven is coming. We have to RUN, Elk. RUN back!'

She was quicker than me. When we got to safety,

we were helpless and squealing and triumphant.

'We did it,' she said, wrapping herself in a towel.

We lay on the sand facing each other. Her eyes were so close to mine.

'Your face,' she said. 'When you were running.'

'I felt brave,' I said. 'Didn't you?'

She grinned. 'I loved it. Your gran would be so proud.'

17. DRAGON

We left the party without knowing we were headed straight for this moment of impact, this inflexible, permanent instant in time. Sometimes I sit very still in the night and think about how we could have avoided it. What we could have done differently. So many little things.

Mab was angry. That's why we were walking, because she refused to get back in the car with France. I was behind her, trying to catch up.

'I just. Told you,' she said, leaving hard spaces between her words like she didn't have the patience even to say them. ' I literally. Just. Said.'

I told her, 'I didn't want to be here anyway,' and

Mab was like, 'Well why did you come then?'

'Because I didn't want to let you down.'

She laughed at that. A mean laugh. She had every right.

'Well you failed, Elk,' she said. 'One hundred per cent failed.'

This is how it happened.

After Betelgeuse, Mab went back inside to dance. I was staring into the bonfire and France came up beside me.

I said, 'I thought you'd gone.'

His eyes were all bonfire bright, and he said, 'Hello,' and I loved the way he said it, like we were alone. And then I kissed him once. On the mouth, but soft and quiet. Before I could think myself out of it. Before I could decide it would be wrong.

When it was done he said, 'I've wanted you to do that for a while now.'

I said, 'I'd quite like to do it again.'

He laughed then. 'I hope so,' and when we kissed a second time, I knew why Mab wouldn't like it. I knew why she'd be right. It could have been me and France left alone in the world and I wouldn't have minded. I would have been happy with that.

I like to think there would have been a good way of telling her. I know she would have been more than happy for us, if we'd done it right. But we didn't. It didn't happen like that.

I was aware, I guess, of the door behind us opening, the sounds of inside getting loud and then slamming suddenly shut. I was aware, but it didn't matter, because in that moment nothing did.

'Are you kidding me,' I heard Mab say.

We turned towards her at the same time, and she said, 'What's going on?'

'Hello, sis,' France said, and he was smiling.

'Don't give me that,' she said.

'Mab,' I said, and she looked at me then, like she didn't know me at all.

'You lied to me,' she said, and she was pointing at me, not her brother. 'You're a liar.'

France put his hand out to stop her, but she went through it. She just pushed it out of the way.

'I did,' I said. 'I guess I am.'

'How could you do this?' she said. 'When I asked you not to.'

'Did you?' France said, and he was angry.

'Mab? What did you say?'

Mab had her hands on her hips and she was breathing hard through her nose like a stallion and she looked like she wanted to fight me or something.

'I'm sorry,' I said, and France said, 'Don't be.'

Mab laughed in that way you do when something is the opposite of funny. 'Look at you both,' she said. 'How beautiful. How lovely for you,' and her voice was dripping with rage.

We just stood there. I heard France breathing.

'And when it goes wrong,' Mab was saying. 'When you two aren't talking to each other any more, where will I be? Where does that leave me?'

'You're being selfish,' France said, and Mab said, 'Is that a bad thing? Am I not allowed to think of me?'

I said I was sorry again, and she just glared at me and said, 'I want to go home.'

'I'll take you,' France said.

'No thanks. Take your girlfriend. I'm all good. I'm walking.'

A nerve at the corner of France's eye blinked, on and off, like a light. It was late. And so cold. Mab was being stubborn. She was making a point.

Such a small drama in the scheme of things. Nothing lasting. If not for what was coming next.

'I'll go with her,' I told him, and she turned away from me, clenched and opened her fists, and spoke over her shoulder, a polite shard of ice. 'No thank you. I'd rather go on my own.'

She started walking and France swore under his breath. He took the ends of my fingers in his hands. Hardly touching.

'I am sorry,' I said, for the third time.

'No. Stop it. Don't be.'

'I'll talk to her,' I said. 'She'll be fine. It will all be fine.'

I tried to pull my hands away, but he held on.

'Elk,' he said.

'Yes?' His face was so close to mine. Like home, I remember thinking. Safely home.

He smiled. 'It will be worth it.'

I kissed him. 'Later then.'

And I let go.

On the road back through the woods, I followed Mab while she talked and I listened. She'd left her coat behind. She was smoking one of those stupid roll-ups and her words tumbled out in these great plumes of smoke like a dragon revving up to breathe fire.

'When did you decide to do that?' she said. 'When did you tell yourself it was okay? Do you know how stupid that made me feel? You're a liar, Elk. Who even are you? How long has it been going on? What else haven't you told me? There are lines you just don't cross, Elk. It's so simple. You can't control how you feel. I get that. But you can control how you act and you could have bloody denied yourself and you could have bloody told me. Why would you do that? Why would you even think about it? Where's your loyalty? Oh my god, Elk, this is unbelievable. I love you. And you're my best friend. But my god do you owe me right now.'

She wore her own rage out with talking. I knew it would happen. I could feel her calming down.

'Can I talk yet?' I asked her.

'No you may not.'

'Can I explain some things?'

'No.'

The road was soft and muddy and she kept tripping over things and she stopped and took her shoes off. 'And these are ruined, by the way.'

'Mab,' I said, and she put her hand up to stop me.

'I don't want you to start talking, because you're going to bang on about something bewildering like entanglement and how everything is connected and two is actually really always three and how all that stuff happens at some subatomic level and somehow excuses you having a thing with my brother and. Not. Telling. Me.'

I think I felt relieved that she was softening. I was trying not to smile at her.

'I'm not going to say any of that.'

'No, because I said it for you.'

'Your brother and me,' I said, and she went, 'Ugh. Really.'

'Yes. Really,' I said.

'What about it.'

'I didn't need to tell you,' I said. 'Not really. You knew anyway. You knew before me.'

'Jesus, Elk,' she said. She put her hand on my arm and I stopped and turned to face her. She said, 'When best friends get better ones, they can leave you in the dust.'

'I wouldn't do that to you,' I said.

'Yeah, you said that.'

'I'll never do that.'

'Just. Oh god. Please. Don't love him better and leave me out.'

She was so close. I watched her shoulders drop, just a little. Her hair smelled of lavender and smoke.

'I'm not going to stop,' I said. 'I don't think I can stop. But I am sorry.'

'I know,' she said, head down, fury over. 'Me too.'

'Can I hug you?' I said, and she held her arms wide open, and tilted her head to one side, and her smile started, just at the corners of her mouth, and I knew everything would be all right.

18. BIRDSONG

There is one side of that instant, and the other. Before. After.

I have dreamed about it ever since. Even while it was happening, it had the fever of a dream. First there is the noise and the impact. Sudden. I feel it through the ground like a tremor, like some deep detonation, dynamite down a mine. I am on my own, trying to get to her, and the sound I'm making in the back of my own throat is like an animal, saying everything.

I see myself crouched over Mab's body, the look she gives me, and the keening, like whale song, like a struck rabbit, something ancient and terrified and wild. The blood is bubbling in her nostrils and her mouth is slick with it in the moonlight like she is overflowing with oil.

I am trying to hold on to her and she is slippery and her noise is deafening and then it gets suddenly quiet.

It stops.

Mab stops.

But she is right there too, this other Mab, standing next to me, wiping the blood off her face with her hands.

Everything about that moment is so shocking, so unreal, that I don't even question it. It just is.

Oh my god, she says. *Is that me?* I look up at her and the breath is pouring in and out of me like concrete, like gravel, like tyre-screech and the gut-wrench of brakes, and I think I say, 'Yes,' but I might say nothing at all.

It came out of nowhere, she is saying. *Where is it? Is all this blood mine?*

I've got my hand on her neck. She is on the ground, and her body is twisted away from me, sharp angles, eyes emptied. She's there and also inches from my ear and somehow nowhere. I can hear her talking, but she isn't talking; she isn't moving at all. We are at a bend in the road in the woods, that short, dark patch of thicket and spruce pine that takes two minutes to walk through, thirty seconds to drive, and that has locked us inside it for ever. It is almost three in the morning. 2.37 a.m. precisely. I don't know how I know that. I must have just looked at my watch.

Mab is shaking and sobbing and she is also as still and as silent as the rocks and the trees and the road. There's a rip in her dress, hip to hem, and she keeps trying to close it, to cover herself, but she can't make it happen, so I lean across her body and close it for her and she whispers, *What's happening? Elk? What is going on?*

I remember the road under my feet where we were walking and the quiet forest noises, all rustle and snap. At the end of our fight, when she held out her arms to hug me, there was this tremor, this deep, wide thud, and I'm wondering what the hell it could have been. I think of submarines and earthquakes and secret underground testing stations and I'm sure I call out her name but she doesn't answer me, nothing answers me. It is the square root of quiet. The bottoms of her feet are black and stuck with wet leaves and scree and I only know that because suddenly I am in another life, looking down at them, upturned on the roadside like the pale dead bellies of fish. I must have taken my coat off because I see now that I'm not wearing it and it is over her and I am shivering and trying to remember where my phone is, trying to remember how. I can't feel my own fingers because they are cold too, made of something heavy and jointed. Puppet hands. I am a puppet and Mab is empty and the noise coming off us both is bone on bone, metal on metal. It's death.

Put me back, she is saying. *Take me back, get me back.*

She is standing over me, standing over her own body. There's blood all over my hands and the shape of her skull is different and above me, she keeps touching it in the place where it has caved in.

I'm going to pass out, she says, but she doesn't. She just stands there, shaking and bleeding, while I try to keep myself from exploding, try to control my wild animal voice.

Things come back to me in pieces from that night. I can't show the full picture, not all at once, not even to myself. There are sounds – revved engine, wood-snap, fleshy thud – and there's the enormous quiet

153

afterwards too, with Mab not breathing, and the trees folding and crumping, and the pleading call of an owl. The noise I make in my throat when I see her above me, and down on the ground. The disappearing lights of a car lift branches up out of the darkness along the leaving curves of the road, and then are gone. The skin of what I've missed seems so thin, like I should be able to reach out and touch it, pull it back. See the car and stop it from happening. Stop it from driving away.

She is lying there and she is also upright, babbling. *Black car. Big black car. Broken light. Shiny mirrors*. She just keeps saying it over and over again – *Big black car. Black-black windows. Broken light* – quiet, her lips moving over the words the way water trickles over stones.

I can hear water somewhere, and the wind in the trees and the sound of cars just a few streets away in the other world, the world before this, that doesn't know, and isn't ruined, hasn't caught up with us yet. I see the lights of the ambulance, blue, turning, and the trees lit then dark, lit then dark. Mab wails like a siren like a banshee like a wolf. And then she stands on the verge, keeps out of the way, just watching as

154

the paramedics come and put their hands on us, all their equipment and us, in the road.

France's car pulls up at the cordon, screeches to a halt. A police officer is speaking to him as he gets out.

'Mab?' he says. 'Elk?'

Then he sees us. I call out to him.

'That's my sister, my – Elk?' he says, pointing, and his whole arm is shaking and his voice sounds like a collapse.

'Let me in there. I was just with them. Let me through. *Please.*'

But they don't. They won't.

I am in the wild middle of a black ocean. Even then, in the eye of that storm, I am noticing things. The night-blanket of the sky begins to thin and lighten, the robin's voice joined by song thrush and blackbird, by wren and dunnock and sparrow, until the chatter is in full tilt. My gran taught me the birds' names, when I was a girl and nothing bad had ever happened.

France throws up on the verge.

I am an earthquake. I am hollow. I am white noise.

★

The dawn chorus testifies to a number of things. The embers of the party, the sleeping bonfire that must be dying out. The noxious linger of burnt rubber, and the sticky gloss-paint tack of blood splashed across the road. My scorched voice as her body is lifted before I am, heavy like sacking, into the ambulance, one fish-belly foot lolling out from under the blanket, and her face, the way she doesn't look at me when they close the doors on us, when I hear them say to each other, 'She is gone.'

19. WATER

Elk, her voice says to me in sleep, and I turn my head and see her up close, all smashed up and broken. I don't know where I am. Every blink of my eyes is a crashing wave. So I don't blink. I just lie there, waiting for all of it to stop.

ELK, she says again, more urgent, more insistent, and then the waves crash again and there is dry land and I am on it, and I'm awake.

Mab is there, breathing and not breathing. I listen as hard as I can for the sound of her, but her body is only silence. I hear my own lungs, ragged, my heart pounding too loud in the room. I am my sore throat, my dry mouth, my cotton-wool tongue. I know she

157

is dead and this is her ghost, but I'm not scared of her. Not now and not ever. How could I be? It's Mab. My voice is scratched vinyl and feedback. All it can tell her is sorry, again and again.

Snap out of it, she says, not understanding. *Let's get our bearings. Where are we?*

Her left eye is horribly bloodshot, blown veins like bright lava. Her right eye is closed up and so swollen it looks like a boxing glove. She breathes in and then out, long and slow, and I can't feel it, but I hope maybe the curtains sway a little, that some sheets of paper somewhere might flutter and lift.

'You look terrible,' I say.

You don't look too good yourself.

She tries to touch me, but her hand goes right through my surface, her weightless fingers streaming through my cheek.

What was that? she says, and she does it again. *Elk. What's happening? Are you dead?*

I don't speak.

Why can't I touch you?

'You're not here,' I say. 'Not really.'

What are you on about? Yes I am.

I see again the great sea of bruising on her, the

skin opened to bone. The earth is turning, the world is spinning and I can suddenly feel the true speed of it. This isn't happening, this can't be happening.

'Oh god, Mab,' I say. 'Have you seen yourself?'

My dress is torn, she says, like that's the worst of it. *I'm going to have to sew it up.*

'Not just your dress,' I say. 'More than that.'

I look at my hands, down my front, at my own bare feet. I'm not hurt. I'm not even bleeding. My panic seasicks back. She is staring at me, her forehead wing-light, almost but hardly touching mine. I am swallowing, but my mouth is still full of water. Any minute now I am going to be sick.

What happened? she says.

'The car hit you.'

It did? I didn't hear a car coming.

'Me neither. No. Nor did I.'

And it hit me?

I watch her start to remember. It is the most heart-breaking thing.

I never saw a thing so close up, she is saying. *It blocked out all of the light.*

'It wasn't light,' I tell her.

There was the moon.

159

'Yes. And Betelgeuse.'

We were walking.

'Yes.'

What else?

'Your shoes were hurting. Our hands were cold.'

What else, Elk?

'You were angry.'

She nods. *I was. With you and France.*

'That feels like nothing now. Isn't it? Nothing.'

I can't find him, she says. *Can you?*

'Just hang on,' I tell her. 'He's coming. He was right there. It won't take him long.'

I believe what I'm saying, but right now there's no sign of him or anyone else. Mab keeps trying to hug me. The blood on her is so new. Her scalp glistens with it like spilled paint. She shuts her eyes. Eyelids like moth wings, papery, trembling, and when she opens them, she looks at me without seeing. Looks through me and far away.

The trees. She speaks like she's distracted by something on the horizon.

Am I dead? she says.

I try to touch her again before I answer, but she is not here. There is nothing to touch.

'Yes. I think so. I think you are.'

Her eyes fill with tears. *Am I really?*

'I saw it happen,' I tell her. 'I watched you go.'

Why does it hurt then? she says. *If I don't have a body?*

I can't explain it. I don't know what to say.

And you? she says. *What about you, Elk?*

For a second, before I tell her, there is nothing. Just a black hole, swallowing matter, cancelling everything out.

My fingers feel numb. I have a headache. I feel cut off, but shock does that. I think I've been in shock before.

I don't tell Mab any of that. I just say, 'I'm still alive.'

A new reality encroaches like floodwater. The world's sounds throb and splutter back into action, the way they do. The early traffic, oblivious, starts to thicken. I see walls and hear noise from a room just beyond us, like giant bellows. Somebody swears. Someone is weeping. A voice is reading items from a list.

Together and not together, through a window we watch the details of a flawless day. Wall-to-wall blue, deepest at the edges. The trees with their arms raised;

161

the sun high and rose-gold over the rooftops, bright and breaking on the mirror of the sea.

How will you live without me? Mab says quietly.

I don't answer her. I am thinking about being strong and resilient and heroic, and about not being able to bear it at all.

20. DOG WHISTLE

I try to tell the paramedics about Mab's ghost, but they are too busy working on her body to hear. I tell Mum and Dad the moment I see them, but Mum just keeps hugging her own arms and listening to the doctor, and Dad is the colour of paper and talking about shock, like that's the end of a conversation instead of the beginning, a thing you go into, like the maze, like that forest, and never come out.

My head hurts, says Mab, and I tell them, 'See! She's talking. Are you sure you can't hear her? She's right here. Her head hurts. Can you help her? You must have heard that.'

They treat me like I'm dreaming. Or delirious. Or

both. They look at each other above me, and then I think the nurse must give me something, or I lose consciousness maybe, because this feeling hovers, all black at the edges of my vision, and then completely knocks me out.

When I wake up at home, I'm not quite sure if it's day or night and it doesn't really matter because all bets seem to be off. The house is so quiet it feels abandoned. Like we are a whole family of ghosts. Mum comes into my bedroom. She doesn't knock; she glides in and she moves quietly. All eggshells. She doesn't even speak. She touches my pillow once, to check on me, doubles over to look and then straightens herself up and leaves the room.

She doesn't see Mab lying next to me. I already know she will never believe me about that.

We are more sleepless than when my brother was born. Mouths shut, eyes blaring. Each of us trying to remember what direction we are going in, all of us trying to feel our way through. Downstairs, Knox careens around like a bluebottle on his own, throwing himself at the exits, gathering steam. I find him in the kitchen, the wreck of it anyway. Filth and dishes. Tiny flies on rotten fruit. It is only days and weeks, but it might have been decades. Before and After. We are changed and this is not the same house. Knox is feral and pent-up and wordless, dive-bombing the neighbour's cat. Arms out and angling like a jet fighter on the pivot while it sits there watching him, bored and unruffled, blinking with disdain. When it catches sight of Mab, it shoots out of the window like a lightning bolt.

Did you see that? she says.

'I think it saw you,' I tell her.

I might chase it, she says, watching it bound to the end of the garden with its tailed puffed out like a bullrush, and turn and hide itself, blinking, under the hedge.

'Be grateful,' I tell her. 'Take its offerings. It's proof you exist.'

Knox is wild-eyed in his pyjamas, face flushed and dirty and hot. I wonder if he properly understands it, that Mab is gone and never coming back. I know I don't. I want to know if he can sense a trace of her like I can, but there's no talking to him right now about that. Instead, I ask him if he's eaten. This new Knox looks half-starved and needs more practical kinds of help.

The counter is a Jackson Pollock. Mab is picking over the evidence. *Chocolate spread*, she says. *Some lumps of sugar.*

'Jesus, Knox,' I say, and he makes a siren sound. The curse police. 'I'll make you something.'

I'm searching for a clean fork and finding only dirty ones, caked with old food, crusted and dried up. Mab stands up high on the counter. She looms over me like a shadow. She looms over us both. I am sure for a moment that Knox will say something, but he doesn't. He goes on flying, executing sharp turns in his aerial battle, his own personal, one-boy war.

Dad walks into the kitchen, vaguely aimless, oddly lacking in intent. He sees the mess, but it doesn't register. He doesn't even touch it. He puts the kettle on and Mum comes down the stairs and drifts outside in her dressing gown, bare feet, hair wet from the shower. I watch her at the bottom of the garden, moving in and out of the trees. The grass is silvered in the early light. Her footsteps run like ants, random and endless, the way they scatter when they're interrupted, the way they full on lose their thread. She is holding on to her elbows, kind of stooped and caved in at the centre, like the camping mattress with the

166

puncture that we slept on one night in the garden, or the woodlice that Knox finds at the edges of the carpet, curled up and gone.

Knox crash-lands his plane at the table, drops onto his chair. He picks up a glass of water and downs it in one. His eyes open soft and wide while he swallows, this noise coming off him like a high whine, a whistle, a thin kind of hum.

Mab sticks her fingers in her ears. *Ouch.*

'Knox,' Dad tells him, like a warning, and he stops for a few seconds before he starts it up again.

'I'm the human dog whistle,' he says.

He is wearing his sweatshirt with the dinosaurs on, and the dinosaurs are smiling.

I picture the dogs in a five-mile radius, hackles up, deciphering his message. 'What are you trying to tell them?' I say.

His stare is sea-blue and very direct. I would like to fall in.

'Come here,' he says in his hoarse, lispy whisper, and for a second I think he means me, and I almost do it. 'I want all the dogs to come here.'

Oh boy, Mab shimmers.

I kiss his cheek and he leans sideways, more

heavily, towards me, and he smiles. Then he starts up with the humming again.

Dad says, 'Quit it, son,' and Mab seconds that. *He is gutting my ear like a fish.*

I am counting how many dogs we know. Working out if we can get them all to sit outside.

Mum's friend Julie is a dogwalker. On a good day, she has twelve on the go. I've seen her in the park with them all on leads. A walking spaghetti junction. I just want to make him happy in that moment. Like that would do it. I find myself wondering if twelve dogs would be enough.

Mum comes in and accepts a cup of tea. She sits down and reaches for Knox's hand and then curls him in towards her, tight to her side. She holds his chin gently between her thumb and forefinger, and looks at him while he picks puffed rice off the table with his fingers, each grain, one by one. Just this once, I would like her to look at me like that, not my brother, but I suppose she isn't to know. If she tried it, I'd probably tell her to back off or go away. I'm unpredictable at the moment, a bundle of opposites, but I guess I have an excuse. When Mum strokes him, her wedding ring glints on her hand.

It occurs to me, so I say to Mab, 'Not one of them has asked me how I'm doing.'

She looks me up and down. I haven't washed. I haven't eaten. I sleep, but then it's like I haven't slept. I am a demolition site. Life is a wrecking ball. *They know without having to ask.*

'Doesn't mean they shouldn't.'

She smiles at me. *That's true*, she says. *You're right.*

Mum says, 'We need to see Mab's family,' and Dad says, 'Do we?'

'They were best friends,' Mum says, and Dad says, 'But we hardly know them.'

'It doesn't matter. We should show them our support.'

I say, 'Can we just not talk about it yet,' and Dad says, 'Later, Jackie, if that's okay,' and Mum says, 'Do you talk about it with anyone?'

'Not really,' I say, which is a lie, because I'm currently talking about it, on demand, whenever she wants to, with Mab. Dad walks through her to put something back in the fridge. His mouth is pressed tightly closed like a strongbox, the way it is when Mum wants to start something and he doesn't. Mab splinters and reassembles. It makes my head spin.

'I just don't think we should bottle it up,' Mum says, like what we are feeling could fit in a bottle.

I say, 'I'm not, Mum,' and Dad tells her, 'You're right.'

'You are though,' she says. 'Bottling it up.'

'Impossible,' I say, and Mab sighs at her. *It's the sea. I know. The whole sea.*

Dad fills a glass from the tap. Mum is staring at him. She looks away first. She is upset with me. I can feel it. I can't believe she would do this to me today.

'What do you want me to say?' I ask her, but she drums her fingers on the table, like now I've asked her a question, she can bring the conversation to a stop.

The water in the sink looks used and greasy. Dad plunges his hands in and drags up a fistful of cutlery. I can see the sides of Mum's face, the lines around her eyes and mouth, silver earrings I bought her years ago. I saved up for weeks.

Mab presses her hands into her eyes. I feel the space between me and everything else opening up again, the great unmentionable divide.

'If you say so,' Dad says. 'But it won't bring her back.'

Mab moves to the bottom of the stairs, her face

170

transparent in the daylight, her starving eyes.

Come with me, she says. *You look exhausted. You obviously need to sleep.*

'I just slept.'

Yes, but you didn't.

I am so tired suddenly that I know she must be right.

'I'm going back to bed,' I say, and no one argues with me, because we are all different now, and all the rules have changed.

I'm not even all the way out of the room when I hear Mum say, 'What were they thinking, walking down the main road like that? And what was he thinking, letting them go?'

Dad says, 'Leave it, Jackie. It wasn't their fault.'

'I'm just so angry,' is what she says next, and I'm angry too, with her. I'm suddenly raging.

'Yeah, that's so helpful, Mum,' I say. 'Blame us. Blame France. That's perfect. I don't know what I'd do without your support, honestly. It means the world to me.'

Dad starts to speak, but I'm done with listening.

'Don't cover for her,' I tell him. 'Don't bother. You're way too late.'

It's like tumbleweed when I turn back. Nothing but silence in that room.

Mab is halfway up the stairs already.

Let's go, she says. *Leave it. Come on.*

And so I go with her and leave them, Dad with his endless washing-up mountain and Mum blowing softly into her cup. The conversation is over for now. No one speaks. The subject is cordoned off like the crime scene. No unauthorized access. You can look but don't touch. Knox stretches and arches his back, and the smiling dinosaurs shiver. He starts the high whistling noise again, and I picture all the dogs in the world, howling inconsolably into their water bowls.

21. LEFTOVERS

I was a kid when my gran told me about the *Mary Celeste*. An abandoned ship, undisturbed but empty, the lifeboat missing, the crew never found. And the Bermuda Triangle, which was some kind of decades-long portal to another world. The *Octavius*, that drifted for thirteen years out at sea. We used to love an unsolved mystery. Until she became one herself.

Come with me, Mab says, because she wants to go home.

I am dreading it. Here is bad enough, but hers will be the epicentre of everything, the eye of the storm of our grief. I see France's face on the night it happened. Trying to get to us and being held back.

And what he saw. There's no recovering from that. I would know.

'Are you sure you're ready?' I ask her.

Of course not. I'll never be ready. Let's go.

When Gran died, people crossed the road to talk to us, trying to say the right thing and failing because there was no right thing, apart from not having to speak. This time, I put my hood up and keep my head down and I don't make eye contact with a living being. Nobody crosses the street to say the right thing about Mab. I'll call that a victory.

Be thankful for small mercies, as my gran would say.

We are steeling ourselves, but it's for nothing. When we get there, there's nobody in. If my house is a compost heap, Mab's is a ghost ship. If ours is a dead weight, hers is a husk, an emptied shell. There are traces of them – half-drunk coffees, a steamed-up mirror in the bathroom, leftovers wrapped up in the fridge. Every room we enter, they've just left it. It's like the two of us have chased them out.

The never-ending painting of me and Mab sits on its easel. In it, Mab is leaning in to say something in my ear. It makes me smile, the countless things she used to whisper. How I struggled sometimes to listen and stay still. We are so many different ages in that painting. From the first time, at eleven, to just weeks ago. It has grown and changed with us and now I guess it stops.

There are other paintings of Mab here. In the one above their fireplace, she sits in a chair, holding very tightly on to a shut book. Almost leaning back, almost relaxing. On the point of it, forever, but not quite. She has the same kind, level gaze that I've seen many times and she looks hungry too, and a bit scared, like she'd rather be fed please, than eaten. In the one at the top of the stairs, she wears a black dress with knife-sharp cuffs that cross the backs of her hands and her knuckles are the colours of bone and lead and shadow. She looks you right in the eye as you are climbing up towards her, and the upward angle of her jaw is a knife blade too, and it's hard to look at that one, because of the time I made her angry. Just that once. Another is in her parents' bedroom, which is dimly lit, the soft green colour of looking up at the surface of water from underneath. Mab and France on two chairs. Hers tipping over slightly. Him reaching out. I doubt any of them can sleep now, under that.

I can't blame them for leaving the building. I might leave too, instead of staying in this house that's so full of the fact she's not in it. With Mab's ghost here with me, I know I'm blessed.

And I'll tell them if I can find them, but I can't say if they'll believe me, or if believing me will even help. The house feels empty and hollow. Nothing living, apart from a wasp bashing itself against the window, over and over again.

Definition of madness, Mab says.

'What is?'

Trying the same thing and expecting a different outcome.

I think she's talking about the wasp until she says, *They've gone somewhere without me. I'm dead to them. So I can't come back again.*

22. ALPHABET

Almost immediately, it seems that life just wants to go on everywhere else. Like an insult. Because it has to, I guess. Because even when you can't stand the sight of it, it's what life does. There's still too much traffic on the high street. Still tourists and weather and club nights and ships the size of Knox's Lego blocks, far out in the bay. Mum still has the radio on in the mornings, filling the house on the hour, every hour, with flash floods and refugees, verdicts and elections, sports fixtures, powerbrokers, the onward press of a world used to loss on an industrial scale.

'Look, Elk,' the newsreader says. 'It's everywhere. Sort yourself out. Get a grip.'

But I can't. I am a fly stuck in amber, a footprint in cement. I wake up in the mornings and I have no idea why the sky is bothering to be blue again, why there is air, and I am breathing it so effortlessly, in and out.

Mum juggles shifts and childcare and her part-time degree. She speaks to her sister on the phone every five minutes, about everything, cries a lot, blames the menopause, same as always. Dad gets up and goes to work and comes home again and reads books in his chair. On weekends he waters the garden. Some Fridays he goes to the pub. Knox finds out at school that the Russians sent a dog into space by itself. He is outraged.

I say, 'Now you know how I feel about letting go of Mab.'

I see Mum give me a look, like, 'Not everything revolves around what you're going through,' and I want to scream at her, at the top of my lungs, 'Yes, though, Mum. It does.'

I already know they can't see her. They never will. Mab has been in the house for weeks now, our invisible houseguest, moving through and around things the way that smoke does, curling up on the sofa, unsettling next door's cat.

The air is before thunder, after lightning. Everyone counting the pauses, each of us holding our breath. Mab watches us at mealtimes with eyes like a stray cat, starving, her left arm hanging like a snapped wing, a dark bloom of blood on her chest.

Dad used to make pancakes and omelettes in the mornings, but standards are definitely slipping. It's all the sort of food he disapproves of, all piled in the middle of the table, for us to help ourselves. I don't want any of it.

What does it taste like? Mab asks me, pointing at some cereal.

'I'm not eating it,' I say. 'I'm not hungry.'

I miss food.

'Well, this isn't that. It's all ultra-processed, post-apocalyptic. The head chef has lost the plot.'

Knox holds his spoon like he is cleaning a swimming pool with it, and nobody stops him. Still learning how to use cutlery, and already he knows someone dead.

He is insisting he used to be other people. Plural. Like more than one. Out of nowhere, he is himself, and also, before that he was this long line of others, all queueing up in his head, keen to talk about themselves. Apparently, it's getting crowded in there. He has to let some of them out.

Mab whistles. Impressed. *Is this our doing?* she says, and I'm like, 'Maybe.'

Knox is watching Dad over the top of his cereal bowl, brows lifted, spoon shovelling.

'In 1536 I was Bati,' he says. 'Wife of the great general. We went to Ethiopia. My husband wanted to spread the word.'

Oh I love this.

'Your husband?' Dad says.

Knox pulls this wide-eyed serious look. 'I was a woman. I've been a woman loads of times.'

He should make a good man then, Mab says. *Over and out.*

Knox's fingers are in the sugar, swirling and swirling. Mum puts her hand out to stop him doing it. 'And don't talk with your mouth full,' she says.

I'm like, 'Really? That's what you're getting? That's what you took from that?'

Mum pulls back to look at him. Her morning frown, interrupted face. 'All I'm hearing is your Sugar Puffs,' she says, 'sloshing around in all that milk.'

Dad says, 'He's a six-hundred-year-old princess. Have some respect.'

Mum's smile is so rare at the moment, it's like the whole room relaxes for a second when we see it. The house itself breathes out. Dad puts his hand on the back of her neck and rubs it. She puts her hand over Knox's. His fits so neatly underneath.

'Darling,' she says, 'you are a five-year-old boy.'

Mab is staring at the sugar grains on the table like they are the stars in the sky. *This time around at least.*

'Where are you getting this Bati lady from anyway?' Mum says. 'Are you googling?'

Knox is not allowed to use the internet without a chaperone. He blinks and swallows.

I tell him, 'You could have asked me.'

My brother's eyes are the colours of water. Surface reflections, quiet depths. You could swim in them.

'I wonder where she is,' he says. 'I wonder who is out there somewhere.'

Mum moves her hand away, and Dad says, 'What's that, kiddo?'

'What did she come back as?' Knox asks. 'Who's she being? Who is being her?'

Great question, Mab says, sitting up straighter, and I

go, 'What, you mean like a dung beetle? Or a beach donkey?'

Charming, she says, and also, *Beach donkeys make me sad*.

'Beetle,' Knox says. 'Penguin.'

'Okay,' I tell her. 'White tiger. Blue whale. What do you want to be?'

She's thinking about it. Mum starts clearing the table.

'What's your problem?' I say. 'It's just harmless,' but she rolls her eyes.

'Isn't it good for us to talk about it?' I say. 'Isn't it just a part of life?'

'Leave it,' Dad says, and at the same time, me and Mum both say, 'No.'

'She's my best friend,' I say. 'He's allowed to talk about her.'

Dad does nothing. He just looks at his rubbish breakfast. Nice family moment sprawled in the dust.

I say, 'Mum doesn't get to tell us all how to do this,' and nobody argues, but nobody answers me.

Mab looks around the room at all of us. *I want to be me, please*, Mab says.

'If only.'

I mean it.

'I'm listening.'

If I got another turn, I'd do it justice. I'd make sure I lived it, that's all.

Knox hasn't finished. 'I haven't died yet this time, but next, I want to be a panda or a pangolin.'

'Don't do this,' Mum is saying, from over by the cooker.

'Are you just going through the alphabet or what?' I ask him. 'Have you got an animal dictionary under the table?'

'Not now,' Mum says to the extractor fan, because no one else is listening. 'Please not today.'

Knox hums a tuneless little tune. He blinks at me through the water jug. 'I'm not here. I am a shark in a tank.'

Dad gets up and puts his hand on Knox's head as he goes past him. My brother's hair is soft, the colour of barley and wet sand. Dad's hand looks like a reptile, like a tree root. The human body is a ridiculously various thing.

Mum is glaring. 'What do you think this is doing to him?'

'He's okay with it,' I tell her.

'He's not okay,' she says, and Dad stands between us to absorb some of the flak. I want him to look at me and let his balloon go, but he doesn't. His back is turned and he puts his arms round my mum.

'He has nightmares.' She talks into his shoulder.

Because of me? Mab says.

'We all do,' Dad whispers.

I look straight at Mab. 'Because of me.'

23. LANDFILL

A car, they call it in the papers, on the news. A car. As if there was no one driving it.

The exact spot fills up quickly afterwards with candles and notecards, flowers in cellophane wrappers, crackling in the wind that whips through the trees long after the flowers inside have died. There is a traffic jam, and a small crowd with bowed heads and low voices, and all this heartfelt, shop-bought junk.

Fridge magnets on a flesh wound, Mab says. *Landfill*.

It all sits there, faded and drab under the leaf mould in that ribbon of quiet road out of town, that sunless, lifeless place.

I wonder if your phone is there, Mab says, but I don't want it. 'I'm not interested.'

I can't imagine ever using one again.

The day of the funeral wears the appalling, slippery feel of a bad dream. Every atom in the universe is lying, and I keep thinking that any minute we will both wake up in Mab's bed and feel nothing but relief. Mab walks with me all the way to the churchyard. I can see the hard line of her jaw beneath her skin.

We're not going to cry, she says. *We're not going to feel it. Just smile like the wind changed or something.*

'People will think I'm unhinged.'

You are. You're being haunted. And anyway, you can act how you like.

So we are dry-eyed and dignified, she and I. On the edge of things, just holding back.

The turnout is ridiculous. People line the streets like she's famous or something. She stands at my shoulder, the blood on her face still fresh and running, eyes bruised and swollen. She is just about the only thing for miles not wearing black.

Wow, she says. *Look at this. I was really something.*

I can't look at the coffin with her inside it.

'You are. You really are.'

I have lost all reason to speak and nobody forces me to; at least everyone gives me that space. I sit with Mab on the bench at the back of the church, sick and dizzy like a concussion, listening, and I hope that there is an afterlife, a decent one, and that I can even begin to believe in it, for her. I only think a god might be useful, believable even, because there is literally nothing else left to hope for.

Our parents are all in the front row. It's the first time she has managed to see them, and Mab draws in her breath and holds herself very still, but she doesn't crumple. Sometimes it is the broken things that hold the world together. It is in our weaknesses that we are strong. Mab is like that now and I admire her for it, more than anyone else. My dad's eyes are sleepless and Mum has worked her tissue down to a paste. Knox has combed hair and a bag of sweets, and he is trying his best to sit still, all that growing in his bones still ahead of him, his sturdy, busy little hands. Mab's parents look weirdly composed and kind of distant, like they've locked their real feelings behind a glass door and if you open it, it could be deafening in there, thunder and lightning, supersonic, the dragon's roar.

'They're so quiet,' I say. 'I've never seen them so quiet.'

Zombies, she says.

'Grieving.'

Prescription drugs, Elk. That's what that looks like.

At one point, my mum and Mab's hold each other's hands. I think it's mine who reaches out first, but I can't actually remember. I've tried it both ways in my head and both ways look right, and also wrong, unthinkable almost.

Seriously, Mab says. *They had like two words to say to each other in real life.*

'This is real life,' I tell her. 'Believe it or not.'

France is the hardest to watch.

There he is, Mab says, and in that moment she could be some patron saint of hope, smashed up and bloody with that light still not gone from her eyes.

He walks in with his head bowed, down a corridor of whispers that say, 'That's him, that's the brother, and the boyfriend. He was supposed to be driving them home.'

Make him come to me, Mab says. *Get his attention.*

But I can't. He won't. He's seeing nothing.

Oh, she says. *Look at the state of him. Help him, Elk.*

Go and help him, please.

'Not here,' I tell her. She doesn't argue because she can see it for herself.

The weight of this on him is too heavy. France is a collapsing star.

Mab saves me. Again. *This is awful*, she says. *Shall we get out of here? Elk. Can we go?*

We leave the church as quietly as possible, a girl and her ghost. Nobody pays us much attention. France turns his head and looks at me. One second on earth, two million years in some far corner of the universe. I think about turning back, but it's too late to do that. France blinks and Mab has already gone.

It is silent in the service, pin–drop orderly so you can't fall apart, but outside the world bays, like it's hungry, I have no idea for what.

Blood, of course, Mab says.

'Like they don't have enough of yours already.'

Not mine, silly. They're already blind drunk on that.

'So what then?'

It wants someone to pay for what they've done.

I feel all the consonants in her mouth when she says it, all the hard stops on her half-bitten tongue. *The driver.*

189

'My mum talks a lot about justice,' I tell her. 'I don't know what that looks like.'

I rewind the dark road, the headlights just past the bend, the uplit branches. I want to go back, see round corners, find details. On escalators and trains and busy streets, in queues and crowds and audiences and my own dreams, I look around me thinking, *Is it you? Is it you? Or is it you?* Always this thin-skin feeling that we could have avoided that moment. That we just missed them, whoever they were, or could have stopped it. Out by less than a fraction of a second, but that fraction set in concrete, turning everything to stone.

'Sometimes I want to kill them,' I say. 'Sometimes I can't feel the ends of my fingers because I hate them so much.'

I don't really care about revenge, Mab says, *or punishment even. That's all for the living. It's not about me. I care more about all the things we planned for and dreamed of. All the stuff we were about to do and meant to have done.*

She studies her own skin, the broken glass of it. She holds herself up to the light.

I feel sorry for them, she says, picking at her milk-white nails, all flaked paint now, like the corner in our kitchen where the water gets in. *Because they know what they've done.*

'What if they don't though?' I say. 'What if they think they hit a deer or a tree stump or something?'

We were standing there, Mab says. *They must have seen.*

'But they aren't walking into a police station any time soon, are they? They're not handing themselves in.'

She shrugs. *They won't pay for it. Not like that. Not in public. They just won't.*

'How can that be right?'

It isn't right. People do bad things all the time.

'And walk away?'

It's the way of the world, Elk. You know that.

'So why do you feel sorry for them, if they're getting away with it?'

She takes a slow and rasping breath that rakes its nails over her ribcage, the bony wings of her shoulders, her nodding flower-stem neck.

Because, she says, *there's no such thing.*

24. RINGMASTER

Knox barges into my room like in the old days when he used to hide under the bed, up against the wall. He'd wait there for ages before I found him, holding himself very straight and very still, like a rolled-up carpet version of a boy.

Sometimes I would only know he was hiding because he sneezed or giggled or yawned. Sometimes Mum would give me a quick warning on my way up.

'Stowaway,' she'd say. 'Keep it PG.'

When my gran died and I was so sad about it, he didn't bother hiding. He lay on the bed with his head next to mine on the pillow and he hooked his arms around my throat. I'm not sure he knew what death was, or that it was permanent. He was more curious than anything.

'I don't like it,' he said into my neck.

'Me neither.'

'Where is Gran gone? Where is she?'

I thought about my answer before I gave it. Knox is a sponge. You say it, he soaks it up and he'll struggle to forget it.

'I think she's everywhere,' I told him. 'She's always.'

He was quiet and then he said, 'What does that mean?'

'Well, maybe there's a piece of her in the stuff we remember. And if she held us when we were babies, somewhere on the timeline she is holding us right now.'

'What's a timeline?'

'I don't know, Knox.'

'I don't understand you,' he told me.

'Me neither.'

'You're funny,' he said.

'So are you.'

Then he drew pictures on my back and made me guess what he was drawing – a car, a boat, a horse, a plane. Always some form of transport, like he thought of nothing else but getting out of here.

'I miss her,' I said.

'But she's everywhere, you said. Say hello to her.'

He pointed at the window and the pillow and the books piled up on my desk.

'Hello,' he said. 'Hello, hello, hello.'

After Mab, he says the exact same thing. I am sitting on the carpet and Mab is curled up at the foot of the bed.

'Hello,' he says. 'Wherever you are. How are you? Is it nice there? Is it full of good things like sunshine and swimming?'

Mum calls him from downstairs and he gets up again and says, 'I'll be back later. We are going to make a cake.'

Mab hangs around in my bedroom the same way she did when she was alive. I think she found her funeral exhausting. She doesn't want to go anywhere today.

Everything hurts, she says. *And I'm tired.*

'So rest.'

I'd like to know what I'm still doing here.

'I don't know, Mab,' I tell her. 'Haunting me.'

If I'm dead, I'd rather just be done with it.

'Would you?'

She doesn't look right – her eyes are fixed on me, not blinking, her face starting to mottle, her lips gone crackle-skinned and slack. *I had this dream. There was a chariot. And you were in it, and everyone was watching.* She shakes herself, like she is shaking off cobwebs. *Three is the storybook number,* she says, her eyes catching the light like marbles, the way wild animals do at night. *Of pigs and bears and witches. Of kings and tests and daughters and sons.*

'What are you talking about, Mab?' Her face is glassy and absent. 'Are you all right?'

I could have been a storyteller, she says, sinking to the floor. *I was getting good at that.*

'Something's wrong with you today,' I say, when her head gets level with mine. 'It's like you have a fever or something.'

A fever, she says. *How's that possible?*

'I'm not in charge of what's possible.'

I'm fine, Mab says. *I'm just thirsty. I would honestly kill for some water.* She holds her hands out, palms up, empty. *I'm just going to lie here. Maybe take a nap.*

She stretches herself out to her full length. Her

hands are by my ankles and her feet disappear under my chair. Her bruises are deepest in the middle, like bodies of water, like a clear-blue sky. Her hands are fists. It must hurt her to make them. There is sweat on her forehead. On her upper lip.

There's a sound from downstairs like someone dropping a tray, but louder. And a vehicle reversing outside. Or maybe a burglar alarm. It sounds urgent. I get up and look out of the window. Mab is really sweating now. She sighs. The bags under her eyes are darker, her bones rising, prominent under her skin. *I can't do this for ever, Elk. I can't touch anything. I can't reach it. Even this one little room is like the end of the rainbow to me.*

I go downstairs without her. Mum is in the kitchen with Knox.

I don't tell her Mab's unwell, or anything. I know that won't help. I just say, 'She's still up there,' and Knox looks around, while Mum washes her hands under the tap and has a drink of water. I guess she just can't handle me talking about Mab's ghost. She wipes the kitchen counter thoroughly, even though it's already pretty clean. She takes her time folding a tea towel like that's a priority, and I clamp my jaw shut like it's a vice.

When the cake is in the oven, I head up the stairs to my room. It's a proper mess still, same as when I left it to go to Mab's before the party, but Mum's been letting me off the hook about that, for obvious reasons.

Amnesty for dirty cups and laundry during mourning, Mab says.

'Silver linings,' I say back.

Mab is standing in the middle of the room, the same way Gran used to when she forgot what she was doing. I can see the line of her body through the cloth of her dress. Her legs, much thinner now, her map of bruises.

She says, *You know that scene in* Ghost *where he moves the penny or whatever.*

'Yes.'

I've been staring at that stupid 50p for hours.

'I hate that film,' I tell her.

Tough luck, she says.

When Knox opens my door with a slice of cake on a plate, he touches my things, the way he always has, like a boy in a museum. He puts the plate down next to me. Mum comes up the stairs behind him, but she says nothing. She hovers in the doorway. If I didn't know better, I'd say she's scared Mab is going to jump out at her or something. More likely she thinks that'll be me. Knox holds her hand quietly, the way he does when someone's sad and he knows he can't help them. It's how he helps them, whether he knows it or not.

Mab loses her fingers in a vase of white lilies. She weaves between the two of them like smoke, lifts herself onto my chest of drawers. I can see where the blood has soaked and dried in great dark patches on her dress. I look at her, up there, half-lit, kind of see-through, like a wing. The bruises on her face are even darker than yesterday. They bloom and pool beneath her hairline. I can't see where they end. I imagine them spreading out across her scalp, joining up in channels the way the oceans map the globe.

'I swear she's here,' I say, once more, half-pleading.

'She's gone,' Mum says. Knox opens his arms like a ringmaster at a circus and wraps them round her neck. I say nothing.

Knox climbs up onto my bed, wriggles close to me.

'She's always,' he says. 'She's everywhere.'

25. SHELL

We are back sitting under an oak tree, dappled in green light, not far from the grave. The little holding stone is still stuck there. No skyscraper yet. No great temple to Mab. Just nothing.

'Finally,' I tell her, as we watch France come through the cemetery gates and make his way up towards where we are sitting. I didn't think he would ever come here. I think I had given up hope.

Mab goes white hot for a moment when she sees him, then dims and glows like a coal.

I knew he'd come.

France's head is down like at the funeral, his shoulders burdened, his long arms swinging. I think of the rabbit-eyed man at Stevie's office, trailing sadness like a raincloud. France drags his grief like he's a carthorse. It looks like it weighs a ton.

Has he seen you yet or what?

'I don't think so.'

We stand up to meet him. My heart is beating like it could shake the ground. I feel suddenly very alone. I slow my breathing like when you get into cold water, to prepare for the shock, but when he gets close I'm still not ready.

What if he doesn't believe you?

'He will,' I say, sounding confident when I'm not.

It is quiet, this arrival. It feels like a funeral of its own. He walks to the grave, crouches down, puts his hand on the soil. When he does, the air goes out of him. I see his head drop, and he says something to the ground. He doesn't smile. Almost, but not quite. Then he glances over to where we are standing under the tree. I want him to look at me the way he used to, like he was really looking, but he doesn't do that. It's like he has left a part of himself behind.

I hold myself very still.

'Elk,' he says.

I am lost for words for a second. 'France,' is all I say.

Mab goes over to him, but I can't do it. I can't make myself move. There is a force field all round him, this fragile sign, do not touch. I'm afraid of walking right into it, so I stay still for a minute. I stay right where I am.

How's he look to you? she says, getting up close.

Tired. Hollow. He looks like France, if France was grieving. Less a burden, I think, more an emptying. 'He looks like a shell.'

'I'm so sorry,' he says. I keep thinking he will come over and hug me, but he doesn't. It is the most bitterly disappointing thing.

'About what?'

'I should have gone with you. I should have been there.'

'You're here now,' I tell him, but I feel cauterized, and Mab waves her hand in front of his eyes and says, *Hardly.*

He looks away and says nothing, so I look away from him too.

I really thought he might see me, Mab says. *I've got to say, I was hoping.*

'You and me both.'

201

Ten steps away, France covers his face with his hands and howls.

Oh, France, Mab says. *Jesus*.

His voice is messed up and half-choked, all water and volume and tears. 'I can't believe it,' is all he says.

I watch Mab try to put her hand on his shoulder, this line of air between them, the closest she can get.

'She's here still,' I tell him, when he is quieter. 'She's with us.'

France shakes his head. He's not even listening.

'She is,' I say.

His eyes are tight shut. 'I'm so sorry,' he says again.

I tell him, 'It's okay,' even though it isn't, even though nothing ever will be again. 'We'll be okay.'

He lies down in the grass with his head at Mab's feet. He is thinner. Older by three weeks and about a hundred years.

'I can't stop thinking about you,' he says, and I say, 'Me too.'

'But I can't stay long,' he says, quietly. 'Not today.'

He doesn't even look at me. There is this terrible disconnection, like with Mab gone, everything is broken.

You wait and you wait, she says. *And then no Frances all come at once.*

'I've missed you,' I say, but I shouldn't bother. France's eyelids flicker, but he carries on staring at the sky.

'I've got to go,' he says.

This is worse than before he got here.

He sits up, rubs his face with his hands. 'It's just so messed up.'

Mab is quiet. She closes her eyes. I want to shake him, but I am rooted, like the oak tree, to the spot.

'Where are you?' I say. 'Why are you doing this?'

'I can't be here,' he says. 'I'm not ready.'

'For what exactly?'

France's voice is flat and featureless. 'I have loved you for so long,' he says, and I should be happy to hear it, but I'm not. It's like I know what's coming. So I just wait.

France looks at his hands. At the sad little temporary gravestone. At the blades of coarse grass and the open sky. He looks everywhere, but not at me.

'I think I've always loved you,' he says. 'And now . . .'

'And now what?' I say.

He just stares at the ground. 'I don't know what to do with it.'

Everything around me feels like it's leaving. I am the still point of an earthquake, its epicentre, and the world around me is just breaking and falling away.

I can't speak. I don't argue.

'I'm so sorry,' he says into the silence. 'Forgive me.'

Mab stands beside him and whispers, *Just let him go.*

'Bye, Elk,' he says, and he walks down the hill in the opposite direction, towards the flat back of town, the sports fields and the industrial estate.

I'm ashamed of what I hoped for. A reunion of sorts, I guess. Some show of feeling from the boy who said we couldn't stop it. Who kissed me, and compared us to the sea. I've been hoping for a miracle, or at least that we might help each other somehow, and be us, if nothing else.

I have lost him then. It's decided. While I watch him leave, I see how long I will have to carry on without Mab. Not a month or a year or a decade, but my whole life, which is for ever.

I am a ruined building, a lost survivor, an island surrounded by sharks.

I dig my fingernails into my palm like she showed me those first days when I couldn't stop crying.

Bite down on your tongue too, she said. *It'll stop you from thinking.*

Except nothing ever does.

26. DUSTBIN

Let's go. Mab stands in front of me.

'Where?'

No idea. Just let's go somewhere else, and she is away from me, walking down the middle of the path, the same way France went. He is out of sight. Already gone. She spins a full circle on her cut and bleeding feet.

If I turn my head too fast, you know there are holes in it everywhere.

'In what?'

This. She waves her arms, meaning everything.

There is mud under her fingernails. The buildings ahead of us look lit in the sun. Life is so beautiful.

There is just no arguing with that.

'You mean the real world?'

It's not real though, she says. *That's the thing. Not any of it. Not even you or me or him. You taught me that.*

'Did I?'

Mr Bore.

'His name is Bohr.'

She smiles. *Whatever. Mr Quantum Physics. Him. 'Everything we call real is made of things that cannot be regarded as real.'*

'You remembered.'

I listened.

'Thank you.'

Welcome. Happy to help.

She says, *You're allowed to be sad about my brother. I mean, I'm dead, but I get it. There are living things left to grieve about.*

'We both love you so much,' I say. 'And I thought it might help us.'

And maybe it will, she says. *Just not yet.*

She tells me I should put him in *the sacrificial pot.*

'The what?'

The dustbin of longings, and I say, 'What the hell is that?'

It's where you put what you want, she says. *To prove you don't want it.*

'But I do want it.'

She smiles, and all she says is, *Want want want.*

'What have you got in there?' I say.

Living to start with. Now it's leaving. I think I want to be gone.

'Do you mean that?'

She smiles. *I was hoping. If he was with you, I could slip away.*

I hold my breath, selfish, fold my arms and watch her. Black eyes. Wrists scraped raw. Raised veins branched like riverbeds. I'm not ready for her to leave any more than she has already.

'Who are we proving that we don't want things to anyway?' I ask her. 'Who's the dustbin for?'

It's for us. To ourselves. No one else.

'Why would I do that?' I ask her. 'I mean, what's the point?'

What you think you want, she tells me, *is nothing compared to what life has in store for you.*

'How come? And where did you get that from?'

Mab smiles. *Life has more imagination than we do, Elk. It has a bigger mind.*

208

I am staring at her, and she points her finger and says, *Do as you're told. Just trust me.*

I picture a dustbin. I put Mab and France in it. I still want them. Nothing changes.

'I've done it.'

Good.

'Now what?'

Walk away.

We are at the bottom of the hill, outside Stevie's office. The rabbit-eyed man comes out of the building, head down, blinking. He's wearing a raincoat the colour of wet stone, even though it hasn't rained in weeks.

Mab is watching me. *What's the hold-up?* she says. *Is there someone else in there still?*

'No.'

So, what then?

'I don't want to go in.'

She shrugs. She is bored of my sadness because hers is infinitely greater. *So don't.*

She's chewing on her nails. They look grey at the centre, the way nails do when you're cold. Her lips have changed too, paler than before, the colour leeching from her surface, fading out like stuff left in the sun.

Want my opinion? she says.

'Always.'

Pull yourself together. Go in.

I push the door with the flat of my hand, bump it open with my hip. It swings back too quick and hits the wall behind it and I picture the dentist's chair, the tissue box, the plastic cups, the greeting-card coasters, all trembling for a second, like an aftershock.

Nice entrance, Mab says. *Calm.*

'Thanks. I made an effort.'

Her smile is welcome. *You really did.*

Stevie is wearing pearls and a green jumper with short sleeves and the kind of trainers you can buy in a supermarket. Her pot plant looks like it would sell its own soul for a drink.

'Who's the man who comes before me?' I say, and she purses her lips.

'He's so sad,' I say. 'It makes my skin crawl.'

She folds a tissue. Grief comes in many shapes and sizes. I think about France, his slow carthorse, being useless, doing nothing. My whole body feels like a clenched fist and so I punch the silence open because

210

otherwise I will scream.

'My mum's reading this book,' I tell her, and my voice sounds weirdly upbeat, like I'm not in charge of it. 'Something about magical thinking. Like a part of you pretending that your loss isn't real, that the person is still there.'

Stevie leans forward in her chair.

'I haven't read it,' I say. 'I mean, I had a look, over Mum's shoulder. The woman who wrote it didn't want to throw her husband's shoes out, in case he needed them. He died at the dinner table. She was right there.'

Stevie looks at me for a long time.

'Do you think that's what I'm doing?' I ask her. 'Is that what everyone thinks?'

You feel it here, Mab says with her hand on her heart, *right in the centre, and at the same time you don't want to be anywhere near it.*

'How do you feel it?' I ask her. She's looking out of the window. Hot, flat sky, bare brick, a scrawny pigeon inspecting the gutters.

Sometimes I feel nothing at all.

She wants to talk about deep time. *Planetary time*, she says. *The stuff you read about in all your books.*

'The stuff you thought was pointless and had no patience for.'

Like watching paint dry, she says. *Yes. That.*

Here's four billion years, she says, indicating the long, straight line of her outstretched arm, from shoulder to fingertip. I watch the bruised soft dip on the inside of her elbow, an angry scab the shape of India on her skin. She points to some southern point of it, inches from her wrist.

The dinosaurs are about here, she tells me.

'On your handy timeline.'

Correct. Human history is almost nowhere.

'Show me.'

She blinks. *Dust. I could file it from the end of my nail.*

'And what about you?' I ask her. 'Where are you?'

She looks at her arm's length proudly, the collapsing veins and splintered bones, the bruises and scratches like symbols on a new kind of map.

Then she smiles. *Knox told you. I am everywhere.*

The black clock is ticking. Mab is lying on her back on the rug. She looks flattened. Hopeless. Her nostrils flare; her eyes are hollow. I can see the taut line of her cheekbones when she turns, her fists budding and unbudding.

If I'm dead, then I'd rather just be done with it.

I bite down on the inside of my cheek so hard I can almost taste the blood.

Outside, the trees whisper in the street, and the sun's glare is forensic. Mab scratches at her palms, at the breaks in her skin like laddered tights. There's this one grubby cloud in all the blue expanse, stubborn and slow-moving above us. A banana skin on the pavement, black and twisted. Somewhere a skylark. High. Out of sight. That car-alarm noise, still beeping. A drill whining. Someone calling their dog's name, I think, far away though, again and again.

She twists her hair around her finger, shifts on her hip, slowly, carefully, like an ancient woman. Her face warps and puckers. I could be watching her through bubbled glass. I put my arm out to help her, but I can't help. I touch nothing but air.

Things tick and shift in the heat. Mab is flickering like the strip-light in our kitchen – half-on then full-on then half-off.

On the corner, a car. Vast and glossy black, with

tinted windows. Slow and quiet. It sets my teeth on edge.

Big black car, Mab starts. *Broken light. Shiny mirrors.*

No reflection of her in its passing paintwork. No upturned nose or heart-shaped chin.

She stops at the kerb and looks behind her. Skinned shins and broken fingers. The shadows under her eyes are deep like night-time water. Gun metal. Bruise-grey. The car turns the corner where the betting shop and the tapas place compete for dirtiest window.

I close my eyes and put my hand out to steady myself.

Are you OK? Mab asks me.

'Not even close,' I tell her. 'You?'

I'm fine, she says. *I'll be fine.* But she's lying.

She looks up at the trees, parrot-green against all that blue. The underside of her jaw is grazed where she hit the tarmac, bright pinpricks of blood set like rubies in a grid.

She pulls at a thread on her cuff. It ravels and ravels. The line of her gums has darkened and drawn back just a little. Her lips are drier than dry, pupils deeper than the place they locked Zeus in those poems she

214

showed me, deeper than the oil-slick shine of her shoes, thrown far from her body in the dark. Deeper than the bottomless well of what we have lost.

27. SEA GLASS

At the far end of the street, France appears then disappears around a corner.

Did you see that? Mab says, her head turning like a whip.

I see his height, the unmistakable broadness of his back. His hair, that amber colour, so hard to describe, so instantly obviously him. I feel that longing in my centre, to be near him. My heart, like a missile, homing in.

He was fast, she says. *Like he has somewhere to be.* She starts walking. *Are you coming?*

'Where?'

I don't know. Wherever he's going.

I keep my distance because I don't want him to see me. The last thing I can live with now is that. I hang back and Mab moves ahead of me so she knows where he's headed. For her, France is never out of sight.

We trail him through the tired part of town. The shut-up shops and boarded-up buildings, people drifting, pigeons squabbling on the street. It's after six, but the sun is still burning. Poor Mary, baked and blinding on her plinth.

I tell Mab, 'Knox would like this game. Like spies or something.' But she is distracted or too far from me to answer. Intent like a bloodhound on a scent.

We're out of the centre now, still walking. It's more residential, just pavements and the start of the big newbuild estate. Gran's flat was this way, and the hospice where she ended up. I haven't been out here for ages. Apart from the construction, it looks tired and dirty and run-down. She used to keep her garden so tidy. A postage stamp, weeded into obedience and crowded with bright flowers. Hydrangeas were her favourite. She showed me how you could change their colour if you put a rusty nail or two in the soil. I called that magic, but she said it was to do with aluminium levels and the pH and when I told her that took the wonder out of it, she said, 'Science helps explains the wonder, Elena. It doesn't make it any less.'

France is moving pretty quick. I can't imagine where he's headed. Home is the other way. An ambulance blares past and at the same time, Mab runs back to me from the next corner.

It's the hospital, she says. *That's where he's going.*

I picture her empty house. Things still in their places, a sudden departure.

Something's happened, Elk, she tells me, and I don't know what to say.

France is crossing the big car park ahead of us.

It's Joss or Jay, Mab says, panic rising, and I see them again at the funeral. Glassy and sedated. It's not hard to take too many pills.

Oh god, Mab says, and she is running.

'You don't know that yet though,' I tell her, but we're both running now, and I'm probably wrong because who else could it be?

The automatic doors hiss open and closed, and the noise of the road outside comes in and out with them, like breathing. France knows exactly where

218

he's going, which means he has been here before. Past the main desk and down a corridor. Right and then right and then left. The walls are blue and white. The floor is this shined and plasticky rubber, the pale colour of sea glass. It squeaks under your feet. There are other noises. Music somewhere, and that skylark noise like a car alarm, and a beeping. Everyone walks fast in this place. All of them have somewhere they already need to be.

France stops at the doors of the ICU.

Intensive Care, Mab whispers, and I try to stop thinking then. I try to make my mind quiet so I can be helpful.

The nurse at the front desk knows him. She nods and smiles. 'Hello, France.'

'Are they both here?' he says, hardly stopping, and I'm so scared right now that I'm not scared at all, I'm just in it, whatever this is, and we follow him in, close together. We have no choice now, other than that.

The nurse doesn't stop me. The room is dark, but electric, like the blue light of screens. Machines and shadows. A disinfectant smell. It takes a second for my eyes to adjust to the balloons and flowers. The cards, like it's a birthday. That persistent, beeping alarm noise is back, like it's been with us the whole time, and never left.

Mab has stopped like a statue in the middle of the room and I see three things, in such quick succession that I don't know what order to see them. Like they happen all at once.

Mab's dad against the far wall, eyes closed. France's back, leaning over, his soft voice. Joss, her bracelets glinting, holding a book but not reading. They are fine then; they are both fine.

Mab breathes out with her hands over her own heart. *Oh thank god*, she is saying, and I am looking at a bed, with someone in it. Dark hair on the pillow, bandaged hands, both arms in plaster, an intubated, broken face. There is this sound in the room like bellows, like something breathing in and out.

I don't know it until I've said it, but then it is absolutely true. I look at Mab, in both places.

'It's you,' I tell her. 'It's you.'

Another nurse comes in, quiet and purposeful. She checks the equipment, puts her hands on Mab in the bed. They don't go straight through her. They touch skin. They check pulse. They smooth hair back from her face. This Mab is solid. She is bone and flesh and blood.

Relief is like light. I am filling up with light.

Me? Mab says. She is staring and staring.

'You're there. You're here.'

How can I be? How is this happening?

'You're not gone, Mab,' I say. 'You're not dead.'

28. BULLET

Nobody notices me. Only Mab, who is standing beside me, and who covers her hand with her mouth. The room glows briefly, like a firefly, and in the glow, the details are clearer, and she is harder and harder to see. It is loud, and her voice is almost nothing, just a quiet scratch, just a mouse in the wall, but I hear what she says, which is, *Elk?*

'I'm here,' I tell her.

But I'm not.

I can't feel my hands. I am so terrified suddenly, I think I might pass out, but all I do is stand there at the foot of her bed. People are moving through and around me and everything is out of focus, all a blur.

The Mab in the bed is alive. Sharp and solid. And crystal clear.

The Mab standing near me says, *Elk*, again, even quieter this time, like she's half-asleep and half-waking, only just beginning to come back from her in-between place, this weeks-long dream.

I say her name as if saying it could save me. I hold my hands out in front of me like a shield, like I could stop it. But nothing can. I am watching it all from the end of a long tunnel and the truth is a bullet. It's coming for me.

It's me. I'm dead. Not Mab.

My voice is so loud in the room, even if nobody hears it. 'STOP,' I am shouting. 'WAIT. STOP.'

29. TIGHTROPE

There is one side of that instant, and the other.

What comes next is too fast. Like the arcade I used to go to with Gran when I was little, the pennies nudging until the whole lot falls. Gradually and then suddenly. Each coin is a bright, hard fact, landing. I would like to slow things down and take them to pieces and look at each of them, one by one, from that far corner of the universe, where two million years are one second on earth. Maybe I will have the time after all. Maybe I won't.

I see it all. The car that hits me first and sends my body into the undergrowth. Both of us there with the lights of the ambulance turning, and France throwing up, deep in the trees. Mum talking and not talking to me, the only way she can do, because I am gone and she doesn't know, how could she know, that I am still there somehow, angry, lost and listening. Her trowel in the earth, and the flowers, and the way she's been pouring her softness into Knox and not giving me any. Knox in my bedroom and my dad in the kitchen at home, all meltwater, holding on to the counter for ballast and forgetting why he came in. Stevie, listening but not hearing. France, on his own then, howling at the grave.

My grave. Not Mab's.

People say that when you die, your life flashes before you, episode by episode, memories one after the other like a reel of film. I don't feel it like that. My life is a well, and I am drowning in it. It is everywhere.

The whole time I'm trying to stop it, it's already done. And once I'm done with yelling, it's all over and I'm okay.

I thought I'd fight it harder, but I don't.

It turns out that it's quite easy to die. It's not even a problem. It just is. You're just not.

225

★

Mab is watching herself in the bed and herself still with me.

Where am I? she is saying. *Which one is me?*

'You're both,' I tell her, and it feels like the sound of me lingers in the air for a second. It rings like a bell.

It's a tightrope, she says to me. And she should fall then. But she doesn't.

She is in her place, neither dead nor alive, only both, until it's decided. The quantum term is a *superposition*. Science explains the wonder, as Gran would say, but this is Mab's decision. My only choice is to let go.

France's hand is on her cheek. She is watching that happen.

'Go to them,' I tell her. 'They're waiting for you.'

She looks at me. She reaches her fingers into her own hand, and it twitches.

'Did you see that?' France says, stepping back from the bed.

Mab dips her face into her face like it is water. On the bed, her eyelashes flicker. They crowd round her in an instant. Her family. France and Jay and Joss.

France's voice is slick with feeling. 'She's here. She's waking up. She's coming back.'

'Go and find them,' I tell her, and I picture her walking into that maze at the beginning. Her calm assurance. Her easy smile. 'Go and help them, Mab. Without you, they're lost.'

She is crying. *What about you?*

'I'm fine,' I tell her, and when I say it, I am lying and I've never said anything more true. Opposites aren't opposites for me now. They are the living's way of navigating the world.

I love you, Mab says.

'Oh, Mab. I love you too.'

I see France's face. The life in it as he looks at her. All that beauty and future and hope.

'You wondered why you were still here,' I tell her.

Yes.

'And I didn't want you to wonder. I didn't want you to leave.'

I know, Elk.

'But it wasn't you at all. It's been me, haunting you for some reason. I'm the ghost.'

I can't leave you.

'But I'm here to make sure you live.'

She says nothing. So I tell her, 'It was the last thing I thought I wanted. But now, I need you to go.'

There is this pause in the room, not full and not empty, but between things. The end of one wave and the start of another. Ongoing. Constant. You can't stop the sea.

Mab stands firm. Between me and everyone else there is this space, as thin as skin, that is pure silence. I'm not scared of it. It is peace.

And where will you be? she asks me. *What will happen to you?*

'I'll go too,' I tell her. 'I guess I'll be gone.'

You'll be everywhere.

'Yes. And nowhere.' I shrug, but I feel certain. 'I'll be where I'm meant to be.'

Can I choose though?

'Choose what? There's only one choice, surely. You've got to live, Mab.'

Not if, she tells me. *Just when.*

The machine breathes for her. The room settles.

Can I stay with you a bit longer?

'I think so.'

Then I'd like to. Can I? One more day, Elk. Let's just have one more day.

30. JELLYFISH

We don't sleep, at least I don't think so, unless we dream about being awake. When I open my eyes, it is early and Mab is already watching me. She has put on a brave face and I love her for it. It is such a Mab decision to make.

I've forgotten how she used to start the day almost mid-sentence. Such a morning person, and me still swimming to the surface, always just catching up.

So I've been trying to decide, she says, *what we'll do with our day. Where would you like to spend it? Like we can go anywhere, can't we? Technically? If we're not really here.*

I shake my head. The feel of the pillow is everything. My room, my home. This life.

'I don't want to do anything special,' I tell her. 'I can't choose it. I just want the day to decide what it is.'

She smiles and rests her head back. The bruises on her neck are fading, the colour of birds' eggs, mustard and pebble and blue.

You're right. It will be perfect then, she says.

I watch my family start another day without me. Mum is patient with Knox. His hair is all sideways and he is full of endless questions and she spends time with him. She doesn't rush him and she answers them one by one. Dad brings her tea, speaks softly, holds her hand for a while and says nothing at all. Small acts of kindness add up in my absence to some broken kind of whole. I have never loved them more than I do now, watching it all happen, the way they are living, the people they all are.

Mab asks me if I'm all right and it's odd, but I've never been better. 'Everything is in the dustbin of longings,' I tell her, and she laughs and there's a flash of the old Mab when she says, *Well then, you might as well be dead.*

I tell her, 'I was going for sainthood.'

Saint Elk, she says, smiling. *Of what, exactly?*

'I don't know yet.'

Teenage physics.

'Grief counsellors.'

Big sisters.

'Best friends.'

Me.

We won't remember this, will we, she says.

She might not remember anything after the crash, but I don't say that because I don't know, and it doesn't matter. I tell her what the consultant said about my gran.

'Not the details. But the feeling. They might detach from their causes. But we'll remember those.'

Dad comes in from packing the car and says, 'Nearly ready.'

Knox has flattened his hair with just enough water. He is looking at the kitchen table through his magnifying glass. Like a Sherlock Holmes of crumbs. 'What are we doing?' he says.

Mum hugs him from behind and kisses his cheeks. 'Today's the last day of this heatwave. We're taking you to the beach.'

According to Stevie, grieving people can feel guilty if they are happy, even for a second, like they are letting the dead down. But when my brother smiles, it's like the sun has come out all over again. From where I'm sitting, the dead love those happy moments best of all. Guilt doesn't even come into it. If I could tell Stevie that, then I would.

We get in the car and drive down the hill out of town. The heat is still biting, but the streets feel kind of optimistic, easy now they know that the end is in sight. Knox is chattering and Mum is fussing, and with the windows down, I can feel the wind, wild in my hair.

They are warm and buoyant, the three of them. My survivors. So much sweetness between them, so much love in my little brother's hands. He puts them on Mum's shoulders. She puts her hand on Dad's knee.

'Let's go to her favourite,' Dad says. 'She'd like that.'

He means yours, right? Mab says.

'Mine and Gran's.'

Where we went skinny-dipping. Oh, I loved that.

'Correct.'

We go under the railway line and down the road with the tall trees either side where the cars are arranged like parquet flooring and the front doors are six steps higher than the ground. Dad parks and after that, it's downhill all the way on foot until it opens out suddenly wide and the pavement heads left or right, above the bay.

All of us breathe out when we see the water and the leaves on the plane trees quiver, the front garden hydrangeas nod and blush.

Mum is holding Dad's hand, and he is holding Knox's. My brother weaves and skips and meanders. He is incapable of walking in a straight line.

He's all over the place, Mab says.

'I know,' I say. 'Isn't it brilliant?'

Mum fusses over him on the way down the stone steps, and he doesn't let on that he can climb statues in a heartbeat, and he could do this with his eyes closed. He lets her help him because he is thoughtful like that.

He's a proper good person, Mab says.

He looks more like my mum than I do, always has done. Same eyes, same mouth and chin. I wonder if he'll be tall like our dad is, good at running. I already know he is smart about people, and that he'll be kind. I think about the ways he might be like me somehow, the things we have in common. And that I won't be around to see any of it. I won't be here to watch Knox grow.

'He'll do a good job of it,' is all I can say then, and Mab must know what I'm thinking.

I'll try and help him, she tells me. *I promise I will.*

You can't be sad around my brother for very long before he saves you. He is hopping about on one leg as soon as we hit the sand, taking his shorts off and walking at the same time. Trying both and succeeding at neither.

'Slow down,' Dad says. 'What's the hurry,' and the hurry is stretched out in front of us, breathing and crashing, the North Atlantic Ocean, the Celtic Sea.

There's always been sand on us somewhere – in our bags and our trainers, our hairlines, the pockets of our jeans. There isn't a grain on Mab now, only mud, only car oil and grit and forest water. She shivers a little in the hot bare light, tries to bury her feet in the sand the same way I do, but it won't touch her. Iron filings to the wrong kind of magnet.

Look at that, she sighs, and it's like the grains

themselves can feel it. They swing and waver. *The world doesn't want me.*

'Well,' I say. 'It will again.'

How come you can feel it though? she says. *If you're not in it?*

I've been thinking the same thing.

'It feels real,' I tell her. 'But I must be making it up.'

That makes no sense.

'Tell me something that does.'

I put my hands down into it, bring up fistfuls, watch it slip between my fingers. It's sand. It feels real enough to me.

'It's warm on the surface, and dry,' I tell her. 'But if you push your hands in, it gets cooler and damper. Ground rice. Semolina. It smells of seaweed and hot shells.'

She turns her face to the sun, and I can tell she's trying to feel it by remembering how it feels.

She's quiet for a while, just the wave noise between us. Dried seaweed flecks the sand like tickertape, the damper tidelines peppered and hopping with flies.

I want to hug her so badly. I have this need like an ache.

She picks at the shredded hem of her dress, white

clouds thunderous, cherries tumbling, blackbirds dipping low over the sand. I pull my shirt over my head, keep my eyes on her, her arms so thin now, just bone and skin.

She says, *I'm glad we didn't know for any longer. Today will be just long enough to bear it.*

'A perfect kind of agony.'

Why is it perfect?

'I don't know,' I say. 'Because everything is.'

We stand at the edge of the water and watch the kids on their paddle boards, the two or three yachts that are out, flashing blue and yellow and white. Knox is already splashing around. Beyond his skinny, wheeling arms, the horizon pulses.

My feet are sinking deeper with each drag of the sea, the water below me pulling and leaving, like when I stayed in the bath with the plug out and a part of me wanted to drain away too, except I never let it; I always got up and got out.

There is always something, in the end, to stay dry for.

I see France first because I am meant to. He is unmistakable. Like the rest of us, one of a kind. When he

236

gets close, I swear the waves stop moving, the jelly-fish hang suspended in the sea. I have to keep my hair out of my eyes in the wind. It's flying about like it wants to get to him first.

Well, that's an entrance, Mab says, beaming. *I give him ten out of ten.*

'Hello,' he says, and I carry on holding my hair back. Just that. And looking at him. It's enough.

My mum puts her arms out and hugs him.

'France,' she says, and he smiles at her.

'How are you?'

'One step at a time,' Dad says, and France says, 'I hear that. I'm with you.'

'How are you doing?' Mum says, and she still has her hand on his arm and I am two things, separate, watching. Happy and jealous.

France looks at her, but he doesn't answer. Just shakes his head ever so slightly. Like a warning. Don't make me speak.

'How is Mab?' Mum asks, and Mab sighs, *Oh, Elk.*

'She's improving. She's not awake yet. But all signs point to good.' He stretches a little, looks around him, like a boy waking up from sleep. 'Mum and

Dad sent me down here. For a quick break.'

'Good idea,' Dad says. 'Rain tomorrow.'

'We are trying,' Mum says, 'for the sake of that one,' and everyone looks at Knox.

He has come out of the water and is gazing up at the side of France, who is dark against the sun. Poseidon.

'Hi,' he says, with his little shoulders by his ears and his bottom lip out. 'Do you want to come swimming?'

'I think so,' France tells him. 'Thanks for asking.'

I love your brother, Mab says.

I smile. I tell her, 'And I love yours.'

Knox is staring at France's arms. If he could hear me, I might tell him to stop, but France smiles down at him. 'Want to climb up?'

Knox swallows. 'Climb up *you*?'

France bends his knees a bit, drops his hand to the floor to make a ramp for Knox to use. 'Sure. Why not. Good view from up here.'

He looks at Mum and Dad like, 'Shall I? Can I?' and when Mum gives him the nod, he grabs France's hand and scrambles up and onto his shoulders. Like walking up a log.

We all watch him.

Knox says he can see the top of Dad's head from up there, the line of Mum's parting. He says it is pretty. 'Like a riverbed from space.'

He can see the lifeguard station and the sandwich place with the red tin roof covered in bird shit and he can see all the way round the corner past the headland to the rockpools that fill and empty with the sea's brimming life. He hangs on tight while France turns in a circle.

He can't stop telling them what he can see.

The gulls are circling overhead and the sky is almost white in the heat.

'You have a new friend,' Mum says, and France smiles for less than a second, and says, 'Thank you. I'd like that a lot.'

He has my brother's feet in his hands. His hair is drying thick with salt and there are patches of fine sand on his cheeks. The shadow of those two across me is a black hole, the sand either side light-bulb bright. I don't know why I don't move straight out of it. Me, who would follow the sun around a room. Knox's hands are in France's hair, smoothing it back from his brow. I think he wants to see his eyes. France looks up at him, the underside of his jaw, his chin, like the prow of a ship.

'You okay up there? All good?' France says, and Knox's hands move down to the sides of his face and just hold there. I know what it's like when Knox rests his palms on you like that. Calm is not the word. Peace isn't strong enough. It feels like love.

'Yes,' Knox says. Just yes.

They look at each other like that for a few seconds maybe, no more. I hear the sound of the water. I watch them. And then it is over.

'What do you say, little man?' France asks. 'Ready to get down?'

He holds Knox under the armpits and lowers him, so slowly and gently that he lands on the sand without a sound. Knox laughs all the way down. He lets his head drop back and it just blooms out.

Before we know it, the day is nearly over. On the way back, stranded jellyfish the size of safety helmets lie melting in the sun. There are loads of them because the water is so warm. The coastguard has put signs up on the noticeboards, warning people about the dangerous ones, and every now and then someone screams blue murder in the sea because one's got too close. I love their silence, and the way they lurk in the water, watchful, like spies. I could be one of them. I am silent and watchful. Mab walks right through them on the sand. They are dotted along the line where the waves could almost reach them, but they don't. Such a tiny distance.

She points at them. *That's life and death right there, Elk. A hand's width away from the sea.*

31. NET

Mum and Dad give France a lift to the hospital. He tries to object, but they don't let him. I don't think they're quite ready to see him go.

'It's the least we can do,' Dad says, and Mum tells him, 'We want to. Really.'

I love her for the soft way she looks at him. I love Dad for the way he opens the door of the car and ushers him in.

It's quiet while they're driving, and Mab hums a little tune. France looks out of the window. Mum sits with her hands in her lap. Knox is curled up on the back seat, his lips blue from the water, his busy fingers, his instant frown. The seawater in his hair has set to concrete. Dad's eyes in the mirror are tired.

'I miss her,' Knox whispers.

France holds his hand and I can tell he is thinking about his answer for the longest time.

'We all love her,' he says, into the silence. 'That's why we miss her. That's what grief is. Love with nowhere to go.'

Mum reaches out for Dad's hand on the steering wheel.

'She is with us all somewhere,' she says, and he nods and I know he can't speak in that moment. I know what he's like.

Always will be, Mab whispers. *Everywhere, Elk.*

I am far beyond grateful for that.

In the car park, France doesn't get out yet. He hesitates. Mab and I are getting ready for this last goodbye. It's coming. I feel it in my chest like a flock of starlings. A murmuration, making shapes.

France says, 'Come up? Please, come and see her.'

'Really?' Mum says. 'Here? Now?'

'We're always here,' he says. 'And now's as good a time as any. I've loved seeing you. I can't tell you how much. I just know they'd love it too.'

So we go up, and I know it's nearly over. But I'm all right with it. I mean, devastated, but at the same time, feeling something like peace.

The room is full of people, and we are almost ready. I can go into this next maze on my own.

'I love you, Mab,' I tell her.

She looks at me, and our whole lives are in that one look. It would take both our lifetimes to unpack it.

I love you too.

She is climbing back into her body. It will be a long, hard road. She will be in the hospital for a long time, and she won't remember much about it. When they let her out, she'll only walk about five steps before she's exhausted and will still have these blinding headaches and a non-stop pain in her hip. She'll be better, she'll keep healing, but not all of her will come back.

In her room, there will be pictures of me on her walls. Sometimes she will sit behind the sofa and touch my bad old drawing of a horse. That's still out there somewhere, it still exists in some way I think, me sitting there and doing that.

Details will slip and fade, until she's left with a

feeling, some part-shape of things, like the ring of wet left behind when you pick up a cup.

She will read Mum's book about magical thinking. Wash the clothes I have left there, because she wants them to be in good condition when I get back. She'll make the cake with the poppy seeds in it, because it's my favourite. She will catch herself doing these things and it will feel like falling, but it isn't. It's what saves her, I think. It's the net.

She will be a sister to Knox, and France will be his brother. I don't worry for a second about that.

France will go on without me. He has to. And she will help him. He will live his own good life.

'Do you know what's happening?' Mab says, and I am not afraid and I say, *Yes*.

I am flickering now like a wing, like the light through trees.

Her eyes are small and pale in the hospital light and she looks younger than I remember.

I look back, once, at all of them standing there together, the people I love, and what I see all around them is the onward press of everything, the constant in-and-out breathing of a brand-new day.

ACKNOWLEDGEMENTS

THANK YOU

To Rachel Denwood for her trust and extraordinary patience. And for helping me untangle all the knots.

To Veronique Baxter for making me laugh and fighting my corner.

To Amelia Loulli for undergoing the seven stages of skinny dipping with me.

And to Jessica Seal. What a best friend. For saying when I asked what I'd ever do without her, "You'll never have to know."

ABOUT THE AUTHOR

Jenny Valentine is an award-winning writer for Young Adults. Her first novel *Finding Violet Park* won the Guardian prize and since then she has written many books, including *Broken Soup* and *A Girl Called Joy*, as well as young fiction series Iggy and Me. Her work has been published in 19 countries. In 2017 she was the Hay Festival International Fellow, spending the year meeting and learning from teenagers all over the world. She lives all over the place and has two daughters.